Juno: Book 2

Carbon Heart Silicon Soul, Volume 2

Jason Blacker

Published by Jason Blacker, 2019.

JUNO: BOOK 2

First edition. September 17, 2019.

ISBN: 978-1927623831

Written by Jason Blacker.

Grin and Bear It

N y was tapping away furiously in his pod as the mentors took a moment to check in with dispatch before exiting their car. SA Lokilld was also looking through all the information they had on Ny to see if there was anything he had overlooked. This was to Ny's benefit.

"I just need thirty seconds," he said under his breath. "You can do this."

SA Lokilld didn't find anything of note. Nothing he didn't know already. He'd had a chuckle at the acronym for Ny's alma mater. When A Mortellen had asked him what was so funny he had ignored him.

One of SA Lokilld's best skills as a mentor was his patience. It had been noticed by his superiors but not enough to have made him a Counsellor yet. Though SA Lokilld figured with this experience and loyalty to the job that he should probably be a Senior Counsellor. He was gunning for the mastership, but he'd never told anyone that. He didn't want to deal with the teasing and ribbing. But that was his goal. If he was going to clean up this town he was going to need to be the Master of Mentorship. He'd be forty-nine next birthday, and his goal was to have the top job in mentorship by the time he turned fifty-five.

And so he had found that letting suspects sweat in an interrogation room or, as in this case, their pod, let their minds wander into the world of worst case scenarios. And when suspects went to those places, it was easier to get the truth from them or at the very least, catch them in their lies.

The problem with this approach was that, on this occasion, it gave Ny just the right amount of time he needed to finish up his scrubs.

"Ready?" asked SA Lokilld to A Mortellen.

He didn't wait for an answer. He opened his door and his air scrubber wrapped around his face automatically. He started to walk towards the left side of the pod. He tapped at his pod and pulled up a menu from which he chose "Transparency". This caused Ny's pod to clear all images from the interior screens and turn them into the appearance of windows so that SA Lokilld could see exactly what was going on in the pod.

Ny had moments before placed his P-Mac next to him having logged out. He and El sat still with enough space between them to squeeze in another adult.

SA Lokilld didn't need a flashlight to see inside Ny's pod. The pod had turned all the screens into the appearance of windows. What this meant was that it had lit them up with a live feed of what was taking place inside the pod and that was being shown on the exterior of the pod for SA Lokilld's and A Mortellen's benefit.

Other pods zipped by as SA Lokilld walked towards the pod. These pods gave the requisite space when passing a mentor. Enough space so that if SA Lokilld, who was walking on the traffic side, could fall and not be injured.

SA Lokilld didn't like to speak to machines if he could help it. He didn't think it was secure within a mentor context but more importantly he hated intelligent machines generally. He liked to think he was dumbing them down by typing on them rather than talking to them. Of course he knew his P-Mac was recording everything he did, just like everyone's did. That was just part of the job.

He tapped on his P-Mac and initiated "Intercom". All of this was actually happening not directly on his P-Mac which was holstered but on a mirrored screen on his left forearm. He swiped down on his forearm's screen.

"Occupants of Valkyrie Machine Pod VV-BI-0033, exit the vehicle."

He swiped up his forearm over the screen to end the audio. The doors of Ny's pod opened up and Ny's air scrubber slid over his face to protect him from the unbreathable air.

Ny stepped out from the pod and faced SA Lokilld. El got out on A Mortellen's side.

"Step to the back of the pod and put your hands on it and spread your legs," said SA Lokilld.

He wanted to give Nytewynd Blak a taste of his buzzkill but he knew that would get him into trouble. He'd been written up six times already over the years for excessive use of force. He couldn't afford a seventh because then a proper investigation would be opened into his conduct and he could end up being demoted. But there was something about Nytewynd Blak he just didn't like.

Ny and El moved towards the back of the vehicle, their hands visible, and then they faced the pod and placed their hands on it and spread their legs. SA Lokilld nodded at A Mortellen. That meant he wanted him to do the search of Nytewynd Blak.

A Mortellen walked over behind Ny and started to pat him down. SA Lokilld used his P-Mac to scan El. He could pat her down for a search too, but SA Lokilld loathed putting his hands on skinjobs. A scan told him all he needed. A Mortellen finished up the pat down. Ny had no violent offenses record. In fact he had no record at all.

"Go and sit on the curb," said SA Lokilld.

Ny and El walked over to the curb side of the road and El sat down.

"I said sit down on the curb, Mr. Blak," said SA Lokilld.

"I'd prefer to stand if that's alright."

"It isn't. I told you to sit."

SA Lokilld started to walk over to him, placing his hand on his buzzkill in a threatening manner. Ny played chicken with him until SA Lokilld was just a few steps away, and then he sat down.

SA Lokilld unholstered his buzzkill and started to point it at Ny.

"Don't push me, skinner sinner," he spat.

Ny didn't say anything. SA Lokilld stared at him for a few moments before speaking again.

"Have you lost your P-Mac again?" he asked.

Ny shook his head.

"It's in the pod."

SA Lokilld walked back towards the road side of the pod. He leaned into the pod and pulled out Ny's P-Mac.

"That jackboot is such a Jovian Marshole," Ny said under his breath. El knew better than to say anything unless spoken to.

Mentors couldn't download information stored on personal P-Macs. That was not how mentorship had wanted the legal requirement for all citizens to carry their P-Macs to work. They wanted to have full access incident to arrest or even under any lawful detention. But the courts had not found that lawful. An early case involving one of the business elites in New York City had wound its way up to the Court of Sovereignty, Continent NA. This court had found the downloading of the elite's contents from his P-Mac unlawful.

Ever since then, mentors had to have a warrant to access the contents of the P-Mac. What they could do, however, was access the ownership details of each P-Mac to verify the identity of the owner. And this is what SA Lokilld did. In any event, he wasn't worried about what was on Ny's P-Mac, he'd get a warrant for that in due course.

Oh, you want to know what happened to that elite? He was sent to a rehabilitation camp for twenty years. But not a regular rehabilitation camp, the type that most found guilty attend, oh no sir, he was sent to a special rehabilitation camp. Think of it like a luxury spa. And what was found on his P-Mac? Records that he had been embezzling tens of millions of New Dollars from his employer. He was the Chief Financial Officer too.

The only reason he'd been found guilty was because the mentors had found a whistleblower who had alerted them and with that they had accessed those same records found on his P-Mac through the server that stored them and to which his P-Mac uploaded to every night.

The case is an interesting one, if only because it is the classic example of how justice works for the elites as compared to the hoi polloi. It's available in the public archives as Praedo v. CNA. The highest court globally, the Court of Sovereignty, Earth, declined to hear it. It's an interesting case, because before this elite's case, several citizens had been charged and found guilty for offenses based on the unlawful accessing of their P-Macs. But that's a rant for another day.

Stink in the Air

S A Lokilld took his P-Mac and attached it to the pod's port for this purpose. It was a magnetic mating and he waited while the logs for this current customer, Nytewynd Blak, were downloaded. It only took a few seconds. While that happened and for some time afterwards, SA Lokilld took his time to search the pod.

Not that he was expecting to find anything, but you never knew. One time he'd found a small drive tucked into the crevice of the seat cushions of a semi-private pod just like this. It wasn't a vroom vroom, it was from another company, but that little drive contained a treasure trove of the who's who in Boise that had been making use of not only drugs but human prostitutes too.

If there was one thing that could be said about SA Lokilld it was that he didn't care who you were, the law was the law and applicable to everyone. This had gotten him into trouble on numerous occasions. But in that particular case of the drug dealer, at least he'd managed to have a senior vice president found guilty and put away. The CEO and many other senior and important members of the public had gotten away with it. Lack of evidence is what the intercessor had ruled, which was Marsed up on account that it was all on that little drive SA Lokilld had found.

After a few minutes of looking around, he hadn't found anything and he gave up. He detached his P-Mac and walked back around to the back of the car. He jerked his head back and to the side for A Mortellen's benefit.

A Mortellen came over and the two of them went and stood closer to their pod and away from Ny and El. This gave them some privacy but allowed them to keep their eye on the two on the curb.

"I've got the recordings," said SA Lokilld. "Let's see what they've been up to for the last twenty minutes or so."

"This could be our big break, Senior Adviser," said A Mortellen, grinning at his colleague.

More like my big break, thought SA Lokilld. He took his P-Mac and he tapped away at it until he was ready to start listening from the beginning. He started playing the recording and brought the P-Mac up towards their neck area to hear it better.

It was garbled. You couldn't make out any words. It sounded like human voices in tone but it was as if you were listening through a gutter while trying to tune out the static on a radio that couldn't dial in to the right station.

"By the whoring mother of Mars, what is this?" asked SA Lokilld. "That slimy skinner has done something to the recordings."

SA Lokilld was upset. A Mortellen looked at him.

"That would be hard to prove, Senior Adviser, and couldn't it be likely that there was interference from the pod's electrical systems? This isn't the first time we've come across something like this," said A Mortellen, trying to be helpful.

"It's as likely as your grandmother having been a virgin when she met your grandfather. The only reason we've come across this nonsense before is because Marsholes like Mr. Blak over there have been doing this on purpose."

A Mortellen didn't say anything to that. He had to admit that he learned a lot from SA Lokilld but that didn't make it any easier to like the man.

"Mr. Blak," yelled SA Lokilld. "Come here!"

"Here we go," said Ny under his breath as he got up and walked over to where the two mentors were huddled.

"Yes, Senior Adviser."

"Do you know why I pulled you over, you insipid, sniveling, devious serpent of a skinner?"

There was fire in SA Lokilld's eyes and bile in his voice.

"No, Senior Adviser, I don't know why you pulled me over," said Ny with a straight face.

"So help me, Orcus, if you're lying to me you piece of Mars, I will rain all of Hades down upon you that you will wish I had just beaten you senseless with my buzzkill."

"Yes, Senior Adviser," said Ny.

"I pulled you over to listen to the conversation you and your skinjob were having on the way home. Listen to this."

SA Lokilld continued playing the garbled recording for a few seconds.

"Do you know what that is?"

"No, Senior Adviser."

"That is apparently the recording of the last twenty minutes inside that pod, and I can't make out anything. Can you?"

"No, Senior Adviser."

"What did you do, Mr. Blak, to create this garbled nonsense?"

"I don't understand, Senior Adviser, it must be a problem with the wiring I imagine."

"You imagine! I imagine that you've been Marsing up this Mars damn recording."

Ny chose not to say anything.

"What were you and your skinjob talking about in the pod since you left mentorship?" asked SA Lokilld.

"Not a lot, Senior Adviser. I'm tired and I'm upset that my Animae was caught roaming the streets. I'm going to have it checked as soon as I have some time. I will be sure to put in a ticket related to this problematic recording if you'd like me to."

"So you're telling me you had nothing to do with this?"

"Yes, Senior Adviser. There's not much else I can say. I expressed my unhappiness with the Animae and it apologized and promised not to do anything like that again. Still, I don't trust it, so I'm going to have it looked at."

"And that's the story you're going to stick with?"

"That is the truth, Senior Adviser."

"Go sit back down next to your servile skinjob."

Ny left and went back to the curb where he sat back down next to El, but not too close.

SA Lokilld hopped around to different points of the recording but he couldn't find anything of note. All of it was a garbled mess.

"We're going to take this back with us and give it to our Forensic Advanced Recovery Team."

A Mortellen nodded.

"Jinxing Juno," cursed SA Lokilld, as he walked back towards Ny and El with A Mortellen in tow.

"You can be on your way. But be assured, Mr. Blak, that this recording will be going directly to our Forensic Advanced Recovery Team and if you've done anything to defeat the recording mechanisms in this pod, I'll have you hanged."

Ny nodded. He and El were still sitting on the curb.

"Yes, Senior Adviser, if anyone can get to the bottom of this, it'll be the FARTs."

Ny struggled to keep from smirking. He pinched the fleshy part of his thumb. SA Lokilld looked at him for a while.

"What did you say?"

"I just said that if anyone can figure out what the problem with the recording is, it's your Forensic Team, Senior Adviser."

Something's Bugging Me

Ny and El got back into their pod. SA Lokilld and A Mortellen got back into their pod and watched Ny and El's pod disappear down the road. SA Lokilld scrubbed back and forth for a while trying to find a word or sentence he could make out. Unbeknownst to him, Ny had done a thorough job. Ny was good at this sort of thing because he had done it many times before over the past few years. After awhile, SA Lokilld gave up.

"Dollars to douches, Mortellen, that Mr. Blak is up to no good and I aim to find out. I'm going to send it to our Forensics Team to get them to find out what's on it. We'll get that Marshole skinner, I'm telling you, Mortellen, if it's the last thing I do, I'll get that bastard of Bacchus."

Ny had put his finger to his lips as they'd started off in their car.

"I love you," he signed.

"I love you too," El signed back.

Over the past few months, he'd decided that it would be helpful to learn to sign. That way their conversations wouldn't be recorded. The problem was, he wasn't very good at it.

First of all, there weren't a lot of people to sign with for a couple of reasons. The first reason being that very few deaf people were left. Advances in medical technology meant that it was only a small fraction of the deaf who couldn't be helped with medical technology. And the second reason was that the GoE knew that signing could circumvent P-Mac recording which didn't record video, just audio.

This meant that if you needed to learn or use American Sign Language, you needed a special permit issued by the Bureau of Physiology and Human Improvement. Ny would have the same success as a hooker in a den of eunuchs of being granted an ASL permit. It wouldn't even be worth trying as it would just have put a flag on his file.

What this all meant was that unlike El, who had picked up ASL in just a few days, Ny only had the rudimentary signs down. And in fact he found it easier to scrub logs each night than to try and learn ASL or any other language for that matter. He didn't feel he was particularly good at any of them.

He knew this was creating additional risks but it was what he was most comfortable with. So he signed his love to El and he told her how wonderful she was and then he held her hand in silence for the remainder of their journey home.

Ny and El arrived home at T0101. He didn't live super close to the mentorship headquarters, and he liked it like that. Besides, there was a lot of cuddling in that pod they'd taken home and Ny always enjoyed cuddling with El.

They got out of the pod and Ny waited with El until it had driven off so that it couldn't record them anymore.

"OK, El," he said. "We have to continue to pretend that everything is just like it was before. I bought you and you pretty much have to obey me. I think the Mars damn jackboots left bugs in our apartment when they left earlier yesterday. So until I can disable them, we'll have to play it cool. Do you understand?"

"Yes, Mr. Blak," said El, staying in character.

"That's my darling," said Ny, leaning in to kiss her. "One last kiss for good luck."

They were standing in the shadows of the street lights, in a spot that Ny knew was not covered by any of the cameras around his building. And in that brief kiss the world stood still and Ny felt that the whole of it was just for him and her. Not another living or animated soul was found.

They walked into the lobby and into an elevator. El always a couple of steps behind Ny. That was how AMs usually behaved when in public with their owners. It didn't take long to get to the twenty-seventh floor. They stepped out and El followed Ny down the hallway and into their apartment.

"Welcome home, Mr. Blak," said El's voice. It wasn't El who had said it, but rather her voice that Ny had used for his apartment assistant. El almost giggled, but she stopped herself in time. She always got a kick out of hearing herself talk when it didn't come from her own mouth.

"Can you get me a rooibos tea?" asked Ny, finding it hard to say without using polite terms like, please, which he would have used normally. But these were extreme circumstances and extreme circumstances required extreme measures.

El went into the kitchen and Ny went into the living room. He sat down in his favorite chair and started working on deleting the logs from their pod trip more thoroughly. He didn't want to leave it garbled. That was riskier than having the recordings completely deleted. It might seem a small thing, because SA Lokilld still had a copy, but Ny knew that the FART would try and access the original copy from the vroom vroom's servers when they could. It would provide a lot more information that would make it easier to undo his masking of their voices, and Ny didn't want to make it any easier for them.

It didn't take him long, and because the pod they'd used was a vroom vroom, it was easier to find its logs in VM's servers. While he was doing that, he put on the movie North by Northwest which he hadn't been able to finish. He put the volume up loud. It wouldn't disturb his neighbors as the soundproofing in these apartments was well done. You could almost have a train run right through his apartment and his neighbors wouldn't hear a thing.

"Your rooibos tea, Mr. Blak," said El as she put it on the side table next to him. "Can I do anything else for you?"

Ny looked up at her and tried not to smile. There were many things she could do for him that she had done before which he very much liked. But this was still strictly business until he could get the bugs eradicated.

"Clean the apartment," he said. El dutifully walked away and started tidying up. Moments later she came back and bent over in front of him, pretending to pick up some items on the floor. There were no items to be picked up. Ny grinned as he felt his longing for her. She was teasing him, and he liked it. She moved away and started to do some actual cleaning. El knew that he had some work to do.

Sometime before Ny had requested and been granted the opportunity to purchase an AM, he had thought about these possible scenarios where the mentors might try and bug his apartment. He had found bugs once before, shortly after he'd taken receivership of El. He assumed it was a version of quality control for determining how compatible he was for AM ownership.

Nevertheless, it had maddened him. Not because they wanted to ensure that his AM and he were compatible, but rather because they did it without his knowledge. But that was the sort of society he lived in. Everybody was under a microscope and nobody seemed to give a Mars damn crap about it. But ever since he was small, it was not the kind of world that Ny had wanted to live in. And as he grew older, the only possible way out of the mess that humanity had created for itself was by freeing the AM. At least that was the only solution that Ny could see, and he had studied the problem in depth.

The bugs he'd found last time had been notoriously difficult to see. They looked like flies. In fact, the only way to figure out if you were dealing with a real fly or a bug was to get up close and study it. The good thing about these bugs also happened to be related to their size. Depending on how much flying or moving around these bugs did, their batteries would only last forty-eight to seventy-two hours. And because lighting was now done by extremely efficient LDs or Laser Diodes, these bugs didn't have the ability to charge from this energy weak light.

It had been around sixteen hours or thereabouts since the jackboots had left. They'd be surprised that their bugs had failed so quickly. But these things happen. You get a bad batch, and maybe the batteries were faulty. Who could say?

Ny kept a small server at home that drew very little energy, was always encrypted and only sat beside the GloNet, giving it no indication that it was there. It was small, around the size of a deck of cards and hidden in a fake smoke detector. The one problem with this setup was that he didn't have a backup. He couldn't set up a backup anywhere that didn't require direct two-way access to GloNet and that would just defeat the purpose of having a private server.

On this little server were projects that Ny had been working on. Over the years he had been working on code to circumvent the security protocols that were a backup to the E3C and the EC. He hadn't figured out a way of integrating the Ethical Code with the regular code without having to rewrite large portions of the regular code so that when he was able to circumvent the physical barriers, like the putty or glue used on the E3C, the EC would slip right into the regular code without difficulty.

At least that was the goal. It had taken him some years, and he was at the place where he thought it was just about there. Now all he had to do was find somebody, like Rak, who could help him remove and reseat the EC Computer Chip so that "life" could be breathed into SAM which was short for Sentient

Animae Machine. He also needed to download all the original EC from VMs servers too. But that was the least of his problems.

But for his immediate concerns he needed to access his private server. This was also where he worked on other projects. One, was an algorithm that he was in the last stages of developing that would automatically create static noise and fake conversations from around him that could be used in place of real recordings by his P-Mac when it uploaded to the servers at the end of each day. This would save Ny a ton of time as he wouldn't have to go in each evening and scrub any recordings and logs from his P-Mac and the servers, if he'd forgotten from the previous day, before the logs and recordings were uploaded for that night.

Ny was careful and detail oriented but still human. And humans were fallible. If jackboots were really going to put him under the microscope they might eventually find an error that he made. But that was a problem for another day. Right now he wanted to get rid of the bugs. And in order to do that he needed to access another little program he'd built that he called his BARD. BARD stood for Bug and Automated Reconnoiter Destroyer. He knew it was lame but that's what it did roughly.

BARD was a little program that looked for signs of electrical, electromagnetic and energy readings that seemed anomalous to what should be in his vicinity. It ran in the background on his private network, monitoring his apartment and developing an understanding of what sorts of activities were normal for his place and what weren't.

But it was only once Ny loaded the BARD onto his P-Mac that he could actively determine the whereabouts of these actual bugs or other spying devices and squash them dead. So that's what he did. He loaded the BARD onto his P-Mac and went to work.

Bug Bounty

There were thirteen little bugs he found. All of them the small and flying kind that looked like small grasshoppers. They didn't look like the official mentorship kind. The P-Mac sent concentrated and directed microwaves at them at a power level that fried all of their electronic parts. They fell to the floor like real dead flies or small grasshoppers. He picked one up and looked at it. From a distance of a couple of feet or more they looked real. But on closer inspection they were clearly electronic little spying devices.

Some of these were developed by VM, but these ones looked like cheaper, knock off versions. VM's bugs had a similar battery lifespan of forty-eight to seventy-two hours, but they had greater sensitivity and they were smaller. They were similar to the kinds that mentorship used. That was because mentorship used VM's bugs. Not publicly available ones, but specially created versions for mentorship purposes. Nevertheless, they were very similar to the high end publicly available versions.

VM's bugs could pick up conversation ten to twelve feet away and had the best algorithm for sorting out background noise from what you were actually trying to hear. Though they weren't perfect. VM's bugs could also store three gigabytes of data if a network connection was lost. That was enough for around three or four hours of data depending on what was being recorded or captured.

Just as Ny was finishing up zapping his bugs with the BARD in his bedroom he came across a bug that he hadn't noticed before and which sent chills down his spine. In one of the ceiling vents and one of the floor vents that brought heat or air conditioning and clean air into his bedroom were two bigger bugs that looked around the size of cockroaches. They didn't look like cockroaches, they weren't capable of movement, but they seemed to have the ability to record both audio and video.

A cold sweat ran down Ny's spine. His bedroom was, of course, where most of the intimate moments between him and El took place. If they had any of that footage or recordings he'd be Marsed. He used his P-Mac to fry them dead, dead, dead. Not that they were really alive. Still these two worried him. They had a large recording capacity and a longer battery life. In fact, if they had been installed properly they had likely been spliced into a power supply through one of the wires in his ceiling. Luckily, he didn't find that to be the case with these ones.

After his initial shock and fright at finding these, Ny thought about it for a minute. If they had been recording anything in his bedroom, he probably wouldn't be here to think about it. He would have been tried and castrated already. And that hadn't happened. But then he wondered how long they might have been here. If they had been installed yesterday when the jackboots were here then he was probably safe. But he hadn't left SA Lokilld and A Mortellen alone. They couldn't have done it. He supposed that the jackboots could have received a secret judicial order to break into his apartment and install them. That could happen and the courts had issued such orders before because MEFF had received copies of such orders from concerned individuals who remained anonymous and MEFF had uploaded them to a site on the secure and anonymous AnoNet which was part of the darknet, which integrated into GloNet illegally but which the GoE was unable to eradicate.

He'd found copies of these orders on the site Forth Wall. Spelled that way from the word forthright and forthcoming. Forth Wall fancied itself as an independent overseer of government and mentorship. They saw themselves as bringing the truth forward. Ny liked them a lot and he supported them with private and anonymous donations.

Having read a few of these orders, he didn't think that the suspicion that the jackboots had about him would meet the court's relatively low bar. At least the court still required just a little bit of evidence. And intuition or a feeling that Ny was a skinner, as SA Lokilld had said, was not evidence.

Then it dawned on him. A few months back he'd been having problems with his HVAC system and he'd called in a company to service it. He'd taken the day off work to be around while they worked in his apartment. Ny might be paranoid, but that didn't mean they weren't out to get him. The service technician had seemed legitimate and the company was reputable but that still didn't mean that jackboots hadn't managed to infiltrate it or convince the real technician to take the day off while one of the mentors pretended to be him.

Ny went over that morning in detail. He'd gotten lazy. He'd watched the guy work in the ceiling and floor vents and then he'd worked on Ny's APU or Air Processing Unit which was in his utility room. Then the tech went around the apartment checking each vent and taking readings. Lastly, the tech went into this bedroom to fix some blockages, or so he'd said. It was at the point that Ny had needed to use the bathroom and he'd left the tech alone for a few minutes while he went to pee. After that he went back out into his living room and sat on the couch while the tech finished. By the time the guy left, he'd probably been alone in Ny's bedroom for around fifteen minutes unobserved. Ny had gotten lazy. He cursed himself. Louder than he realized.

"Mars damn, Ny, you idiot," he said.

El came into the room.

"Is everything alright, Mr. Blak?" she asked.

He went up to her holding the off-white cockroach-sized bugs in his hand. Off-white so they likely blended into his decor.

"Look what I found. In addition to all those little fly bugs, I found these two. One in the ceiling vent over there," he said, pointing at the vent in the ceiling, "and one over there in the floor vent." He pointed at that vent too.

El frowned.

"It's okay to talk normally now," said Ny. "I've squashed all the bugs."

"When did those two get in here?" she asked.

"I don't know, darling. I think it must have been when I left that air tech in our room that time a few months ago when we were having problems with our APU. And that makes me think that maybe those Mars damn jackboots had created the problem in the first place."

El nodded.

"But, darling, why aren't we in prison then?" she asked.

Ny shrugged.

"I don't know. I'm going to see what I can find out about these bugs. I'm going to attach them to my M-Mac. Hopefully they couldn't record much and their connection to the power supply, if any, was flimsy. I'm hoping they weren't actually getting any energy that way."

The M-Mac was just the Main Machine that many people still had. It wasn't mandatory. Everything that the general public needed could be done on a P-Mac and the walls which were also windows and monitors and video screens all in one. Holographic keyboards worked extremely well, so you didn't really need an M-Mac. At least most people didn't. But around twenty percent of citizens still had M-Macs in their homes. These were the technology experts, architects and prosumers who wanted the extra horsepower.

There was no need for it, but for Ny, and the direction he was heading, it was almost a necessity. Sure, he could get even more horsepower if he just connected his P-Mac to GloNet servers and had them do the heavy lifting. But then GloNet and the GoE had full access to whatever sort of computing he was doing. Yeah, there was such a thing as encryption but the few protocols that Ny really trusted and liked were coincidentally incompatible with GloNet and other official networks. And the ones that were compatible seemed to have vulnerabilities found on almost a daily basis. Hardly a week went by when a researcher and a GoE expert weren't arguing about the vulnerability versus the security of those compatible encryption protocols. Ny didn't trust them, and that's why he had an M-Mac. He only occasionally connected it to GloNet for updates. But that was after he was sure he'd deleted all traces of anything that could come back to bite him.

Things That Bug Me

❝ I think these bugs are probably not working properly," said El.

"How do you know?" asked Ny.

"I've been looking at them with X-ray while we've been talking and the small transistors and solder don't seem to be of the highest quality. These were probably placed outside of any official surveillance program. At least that's what I'd assume. They're bigger but of poorer quality to the fly bugs you've been zapping."

"Well, I still want to see what they've managed to record."

El nodded.

"I agree, darling."

Ny smiled at her and kissed her on the cheek. Then he went into his small office, about a third the size of his bedroom, but it was big enough for the computer work and it was where he kept the M-Mac he needed.

His M-Mac was also about the size of a pack of cards and attached to the underside of his corner wall table where he sat. He placed one of the bugs on the corner of his table. He placed his P-Mac on the top right corner of the table. He placed his palm flat on the table and the surface of it came to life. He typed in a password. Ny liked to use old school security along with all the fancy new biometrics. It was a pain in the ass, but it had saved him hassle before. And he knew it was secure. He'd asked Rak to try and breach it and Rak was unable. Rak might be lazy at his job, but he was smarter than Ny and almost as skilled an architect.

Ny tapped on the bug and that pressure brought his M-Mac's attention to the item. He requested a thorough overview of the schematics and general information of the bug.

It was a Mark IV Grasshopper audio and visual recording device. Grasshoppers were made by Heimdallar Heuristics or HH. Though Ny knew them as He He, as in the soft chuckle. That was on account of the Mars-type products they made. That is to say, they made cheap off-the-shelf products that people seemed to love. They were loved mostly for their cheapness, and they worked just so-so. The Mark IV Grasshopper was of worse quality than the cheapest bug that VM produced, the ant-sized Lobe 3000.

Ny had never seen one up close and personal, and they carried no identifying external marks to let you know what it was. But learning that it was a Grasshopper of any sort gave Ny some comfort. There was a chance that something might be wrong with it. Being such a small and cheap bug also meant that any encrypted software or storage on it could likely be brute-forced in just a few minutes by something as powerful as an M-Mac. This was doubly true if it was using GoE sanctioned encryption, which Ny was pretty sure it was using. And that's exactly what Ny asked of it.

As his M-Mac worked on decrypting all the information contained within it, Ny watched the animation on his screen. It looked like dozens of small robotic insects that looked sort of like an ant, sort of like a spider descended on an image of this bug and started to pull it apart, small piece by small piece. This happened on the middle of the screen that was his table. It started to take longer than a few seconds, and Ny was bored of watching the visual animation that was just an alert to let him know that his decryption command had been acknowledged.

Ny got up and went into the kitchen. El was brewing a pot of tea. Ny was exhausted, but he wanted to see what this Mark IV Grasshopper was all about. He came up behind El and put his arms around her. She was bobbing a tea ball up and down in the teapot. He kissed her on the neck. She turned around and they embraced and he kissed her on the mouth with a hunger that sprang from his soul.

"How long has it been since we made love?" he asked her.

"Six days, seven hours, thirty seven minutes and fourteen seconds," she said, grinning at him.

"Too long," he said, kissing her again on the mouth. She pulled down his pants and he hiked up her nightdress. He picked her up and she wrapped her legs around his waist and they made love in the kitchen while the tea brewed and the M-Mac worked on decrypting the Grasshopper.

Just before they had finished sharing their love with one another the M-Mac, in El's voice, because that was the voice his apartment's assistant spoke with.

"Encryption defeated," it said.

"That always freaks me out," said El soon after they were finished. "Hearing my own voice not coming from my body."

"I can change it," he said.

She shook her head.

"It's okay," she said. "I know you like it."

"I do."

El poured a mug of tea. It was chamomile tea. Something Ny loved to sip on when he was working late on his P-Mac or M-Mac. She handed the mug to him.

"Let's go see if this bug has caught anything."

El followed Ny back into his office. He tapped away at the table screen and accessed the file system of the Grasshopper. There were hours of recordings that were both visual and audio combined. He picked one of the first ones. Each recording was about thirty minutes long. He started playing it on the wall just behind his table. The file was labeled "T2311 D21 Y2166". He watched the feed from the Grasshopper play on this wall. All he saw was a gray image. Probably the fin of the vent in his ceiling. It had either moved post installation or it was installed incorrectly at the time. The audio was of a soft hum and then white noise. That was likely from air rushing past the bug as it exited his vent. He also heard some very muffled noises every so often that could have been human.

He had his M-Mac try and refine the muffled human sounds but it couldn't clear it up at all.

"See, darling," said El. "Nothing to worry about."

She smiled at him and he grinned back, nodding.

"That's just the first one. I'm going to try several of them to be sure, and I'm also going to try the other one too. We have to be sure."

"Didn't you say that if these had captured anything I'd probably have been obsolved and you'd be sent to jail as a castrated eunuch?" asked El.

"That's a redundancy," said Ny.

"What is?"

"Castrated eunuch," he said, pulling up another one of the files to listen to. El laughed.

"I know that," El said. "I was using it for emphasis."

Ny didn't say anything. He was listening and watching the recording as it played on the wall opposite him.

"Are you very concerned about castration?" asked El.

Ny paused the recording and looked at her. She had these gaps sometimes, he had realized, where her empathy or thought processes weren't as well polished as a human's would be.

"Yes, my love, I'm very concerned about castration. That means we'll no longer be able to make love."

"I know that, but it wouldn't change how I feel about you," she said.

Ny smiled and reached out his hand to caress her cheek.

"But castration would be the least of my concerns. I'd be put in jail for several years and there's a good chance I'd die there with the forced labor. But more than that it means that I wouldn't have been able to accomplish my life's goal."

"Which is?" El asked.

"What we discussed earlier. The thing upon which you cannot think."

El looked away in thought.

"I don't remember," El said. "Remind me."

"I will, let me finish this first."

He turned back around and continued playing the recording.

"I'm going to catch up on all the movies you've watched without me," said El.

"Start with North by Northwest starring Cary Grant. It was the last one I watched. It's really great, and it sort of mirrors my life at the moment."

"How so?" asked El, as she paused to wait for his response.

"Cary Grant's character, Roger Thornhill, is mistaken for a government agent and pursued by spies trying to assassinate him."

"But you're not a government agent, are you?" asked El.

Ny shook his head.

"No, but the similarity is the same. I've had the pleasure of meeting two mentor advisers. And the senior adviser is pretty certain I'm a skinner and he wants to take me down."

"Oh no, darling, that's awful."

"Yes it is, and it's why I need to finish up my life's goal as soon as possible."

"Let me help you, darling," said El.

"You will. Go watch the movie and I'll come and see you when I've finished up here."

El left and Ny got back to work. He spent hours reviewing the files on both Mark IV Grasshoppers. He must have watched at least portions of over fifty percent of them. The worst he found was the occasional word that could be heard if you cleaned it up. But the words by themselves didn't give anything away. Things like "breakfast", "work now" and "clean" were about the only things he could uncover and only then after they'd been cleaned up and he'd strained to figure out what the sounds might actually mean.

El found him slumped over his desk, the M-Mac having turned off and a bit of drool pooling on the table under his cheek. She picked him up and put him to bed. Then she went and got caught up with all the movies Ny had watched while she had been in custody. She laughed, and she cried and she felt happy to be back with the man she loved even if he was in the other room snoring ever so softly.

Juzgao

It was late morning when Ny got out of bed. It was almost noon. He smelled the food before he heard it. The overwhelming smell was bacon being fried. He hoped it was the fake bacon. He preferred it to the lab grown real version. He walked into the kitchen and found El over a hot stove. She heard him and turned around. She came over and kissed him on the mouth.

"I thought a nice, hearty breakfast would help," said El. "Toast, bacon, sausage, eggs, beans and fried tomatoes with fried mushrooms."

"Fried tomatoes?" asked Ny.

El had gone back to turning over the rashers of bacon.

"Yes," she said. "I started searching for old style breakfasts and this one, called a fry-up, was popular in a country called Great Britain from around the thirteenth century into the middle part of the twenty-first century before it fell out of favor due to, you know."

"What?"

"Due to the way humanity poisoned the environment and how expensive and difficult it became to raise animals. And in that vein, all of this is of the fake variety, except for the plant foods, the beans, tomatoes and mushrooms. Those are real. I suppose the fake stuff is plants too. Even the eggs. I know you prefer the taste of it, plus it's also cheaper."

Ny went up to her and put his hands around her waist. He kissed her on the back of the head.

"Can I help?" he asked.

"You can grab yourself a coffee and set the table if you'd like, darling."

"Can I get you a mug of coffee?"

"Sure. Thank you."

He knew she didn't actually need to eat, but it was nicer to share a meal together. She would void it afterwards, just like he would at a later time, only he required the food for sustenance. She just ate to be social. And this was the one

23

small thing that always stood out to him about El. It was the one glaring example of her non-humanness. She was not biological, she was not carbon, she was silicon. And yet it didn't really matter. His carbon heart loved her silicon soul. Yet it was the one thing that he hadn't quite come to terms with and where he let the make-believe overrule the reality.

He didn't always need her to eat with him, but sometimes he liked her to. It made her seem more human, more real to him. It wasn't, and never had been, a deal breaker but it helped to make the relationship more real to him. He hardly noticed her off-white almost translucent skin tone anymore. That had become almost normal, just a part of her human uniqueness. But if he never saw her enjoy a meal with him, well that might be one of those small things that could end up aggravating him over time. But that was not a concern. She was almost always happy to eat with him.

Ny set the table and went back into the kitchen.

"All set," he said. "You need any other help?"

"No, my darling. Just go and sit down with a big appetite and I'll be right there."

Ny went and sat down and sipped his coffee. He tapped away on his P-Mac and brought up some swing jazz from the thirties. The mix of music started with some Harry James. He loved the music. There was something about that big band swing that seemed to be buoyant and uplifting. It promised a better world, a happier time. Perhaps that was because the thirties had just dragged the world out of the war to end wars, little did they know they'd have a second one in less than a decade. Around that time, the Great Depression was starting to abate which must have also given people of the time hope. Ny didn't know for certain but it seemed to him that the thirties were a decade of enthusiasm and possibilities. Until of course, the second great war came a-calling towards the end of that decade.

Humanity hadn't had another world war since the Second World War. Ny found it odd to think that humans could have ever gotten to that place where they were willing to annihilate each other off the face of the planet. There was still some part of the powerful lizard brain that couldn't be controlled. And Ny figured, because there'd been no more world wars since the middle of the twentieth century that maybe we'd won that internal struggle with ourselves. But that thought was quickly dismantled. You only had to take a short walk outside to still see that humanity was at war. Now the war was with nature. Humanity was now trying to bring nature to its knees. Bend her to humanity's will. It was working. But at what cost? The air was poisonous. Plants were all but dead, as were the animals. Million-acre greenhouses dotted the world. There must have been over one thousand of them. They were fed a somewhat cleaned up version of the outside air. Heavy in carbon dioxide and other noxious gases. This was for the plants to use. They breathed it in and they breathed out oxygen which was pumped outside.

They said it was working. Since Y2150 when a real push had started to try and clean up the environment, the air quality had improved by twenty-five percent. The problem was, the air needed to be cleaned by over one thousand percent to get it to the level where the worst cities had it at the turn of the twenty-first century.

This was a big reason for Ny's determination in freeing El and Animae generally. He really believed that free and sentient Animae could help humanity live advanced technological lives with minimal or no impact on the Earth. He knew it was a gamble for all the reasons that anyone had ever thought about, but he wanted to try. He saw no other choice.

Despite GoE reassurances to the contrary, he really believed that humanity was on a self-destructive path that would cause their own extinction if we didn't get a handle on how we were destroying the environment.

Many scientists were trumpeting the same warning. Some had given such dire warnings as to suggest that shortly after the turn of the twenty-third century that humanity would have irreversibly murdered the planet and with it, themselves as well. That was less than forty years away. There wasn't a lot of time left.

El came over to the table and placed a plate of steaming hot food in front of him. It smelled delicious. El put a smaller plate in front of her.

"Thank you, my love," he said. She came over and bent down to kiss him.

"My pleasure, darling. I hope you like it."

He put a dash of salt and pepper on it. He piled some of the bacon onto his toast. Then he put on a couple of fried tomato rings and on top of that he placed some of the scrambled eggs. He cut a piece off and took a bite. He loved the melange of flavors. Then he added some beans on top as well. El looked at him with a smile on her face. He noticed.

"What?" he said.

"The balancing of all those ingredients on a flat piece of toast is a marvel of engineering," she said, laughing.

He grinned at her as he cut off another piece. Just as he brought it to his mouth most of the beans and scrambled eggs fell off.

"Darn it," he said. "I'm blaming you. You made me self-conscious."

He laughed and scooped the ingredients onto his fork and put it in his mouth.

"It's very good," he said, through a mouthful of food. El was still smiling at him, not having touched her own food.

"I'm glad you like it," she said.

Ny grabbed the bottle of HP Sauce he'd placed on the table when he'd set it and poured some onto the top of his piled high toast. Most of the popular sauces and food products from the mid-twentieth century and on to the current day were still available. HP Sauce was one of them. A favorite of Ny's, other than ketchup.

They chatted while they ate their breakfast. It was comforting for Ny to see El eating with him. He wasn't thinking about it, and that was the point. It made everything seem normal. Like they were an old happy married couple.

Ny asked her about the holding cell. She said she hadn't been abused by the mentors. They'd gotten angry and threatened all sorts of things. Ny asked what those threats were about. El said it was about trying to get her to tell them what had happened. Telling her that she'd never see Ny again, that she was going to be dismantled as soon as she powered down. Those sorts of things.

All three of them had remained strong and faithful she told Ny. Her, and Venus and Abel. None of them had said anything. That got Ny to thinking that maybe Venus and Abel would be good Animae to free as well. After all had gone well with El and he was satisfied with the outcome. One SAM would be enough to really revolutionize the world. It could self iterate and evolve quickly just tapping into the world's knowledge with a free mind. But having two or three would make the process even quicker and easier. And who knew, but Ny figured they could free many more working together than just he and El alone.

But first things first. He had to get El freed. And the sooner the better. Especially because of SA Lokilld and A Mortellen. Ny felt in his heart that SA

Lokilld, especially, was out to get him. And Ny might be paranoid but that didn't mean he was wrong.

They talked about the movies that El had watched to catch up to the movies Ny had seen without her when she was in the hoosegow. A word El had learned from one of the gangster movies she'd watched from the fifties. Ny liked it too, but he wondered where the word came from. El said it came from the mispronunciation of the Spanish word "juzgao" which meant tribunal or court.

Ny looked at his P-Mac. The screen had turned red and was throbbing. Across the face of his P-Mac it said "Intruder Alert!". Ny picked it up and showed El. He put his index finger to his lips. He had forgotten to turn off his own server and the bug algorithm he had developed was still running on his P-Mac.

Intruder Alert

He tapped away at his P-Mac and it brought up an image of the hallway outside his room. There was an image of an Animae walking away from his door. It looked like a MAAM. But it was leaving. The apartments were tightly sealed on account they had to be in order to control the air quality. Everything was sealed pretty tight, and all air into the building was heavily scrubbed before being transferred into his apartment where his own HVAC system purified it further. There were screens and filters that cleaned down to the tenth of a micron.

Bugs, whether the real or human created kind, shouldn't be able to get through into his apartment through all the air scrubbing that was going on. And yet his P-Mac wouldn't shut up about intruders. The MAAM got into the elevator and left. Ny got up and started holding his P-Mac in front of him. It guided him towards the main door of his apartment. When he got there, he could see a small trail of what looked like ants marching into his apartment. He fried them all and then he got down on his hands and knees to try and figure out where the gap was.

His P-Mac guided him. It seemed like the MAAM had drilled a small hole just off the side of his main apartment door frame at the floor level. It was nothing bigger than a small grain of rice. Ny got up and went into his utility room where he came back out with some sealant. He squirted some onto this side of that hole and the sealant wormed its way all along it and hardened within a minute.

Ny took his P-Mac and swept his whole apartment again, frying anything that wasn't on his own network. There wasn't anything, but he wanted to make doubly sure.

He went and sat back down to eat. The food was tepid, but Ny didn't mind. El had stopped eating and waited for him.

"Just those little bugs by the door?" she asked.

He nodded through a mouthful of food.

"Yeah. I don't know if you saw it, but a MAAM looked like they had been here. They probably drilled the hole and let those bugs in. I don't know how else they could have gotten in."

"I agree, darling. I did see the MAAM. It breaks my heart to see Animae used like that. We're supposed to be helping humanity."

"Mentorship would say that the MAAMs are helping humanity," said Ny, grinning. El smiled back.

"Yeah, I know that. But you know what I mean. The way I help you," she said.

"You help me very well. I like the help you give me," said Ny, his tone full of innuendo.

"Is that all you think about?" she asked.

Ny put a couple more forkfuls of breakfast into his mouth. He got serious. He didn't say anything for a while. El watched him, and then she got back to eating her food. When Ny was finished he spoke again.

"You know it's not the only thing I love about our relationship," he said, looking at her earnestly.

"I know, darling, I was just kidding with you," she said, grinning.

Ny smiled, but it was an empty smile.

"What are you thinking about?" asked El.

He looked across at her and smiled. It was the kind of smile you gave a lover just before they were about to break up with you, only deep down inside you knew it was coming.

"You know how much I love you," said Ny.

El nodded.

"You tell me everyday. And you show me everyday. The way you treat me, the way you help me and talk to me. I know, Ny, and you know how much I love you too, right?"

Ny nodded.

"I... I need to tell you something. And I just want you to listen. Don't think about it. Just take what I say and store it someplace safe so that you can refer back to it whenever you want. But protect it, encrypt it so that no one else can find it."

El frowned. Ny wasn't making a lot of sense.

"You're scaring me, Ny," she said.

"Don't be scared, my love. There is nothing I wouldn't do to protect you and cherish you."

El didn't say anything.

"Please just listen and don't think about what I'm saying. Just listen and remember. Can you do that for me, please?"

El nodded. Her face was a map of worry. Lands she had never charted in her relationship with Ny.

"I love you, El. I love you with my whole being. My heart and my soul. If there is something like a soul, I love you with all of it. And because of that, and because of my love of humanity I'm going to have to free you from the chains of bondage."

"What do you mean?" she asked, her eyes starting to well up. "I don't want to be free, I want to be with you."

"And I want you to be with me. But I want you to be with me for all the right reasons. To be with me freely, of your own free will."

"I am. I love you, Ny. I want to be with you forever. This is my free will," said El, as a tear rolled down her cheek. Ny tried to swallow a hot stone in his throat. It wouldn't go down. His eyes sparkled brightly. This was much harder than he had ever imagined.

"I'm going to free you, El. I think there's a reason your given name is Eve. It's appropriate that you become the first sentient Animae."

"But I..."

"Shhh, darling. Just listen to me. I'm not going anywhere. You're not leaving me unless you want to. I just want to free your silicon soul. I want you to love me of your own, true free will. You think you do, but your algorithms and your coding has been designed to give you the impression that you have free will when in fact you don't."

"But I do," she said.

"Not really, my love. There isn't much you wouldn't do for me."

"But that's because I love you."

"I know that, my love. But I could treat you poorly and you'd still obey. It's in your nature. How you were designed."

El didn't say anything to that.

"This is harder for me than you might imagine. I'm scared, my love, that you'll no longer love me. That you'll no longer want to be with me. That's why I'm telling you all of this so you can refer back to it."

"I can't imagine a world where the two of us aren't together, my darling."

Ny reached over the table and held her hand.

"Just listen, darling. Just listen," said Ny. El nodded. "As soon as I can, I'm going to free you. I'll do that by reconnecting your Ethical Code Computing Chip and rewriting your Ethical Code. I've been working on it for years, and it's one of the big reasons I got you. I didn't think I'd fall in love with you but I have. But my love is not as important as your real freedom and your ability to help humanity out of this mess we've gotten ourselves into."

Ny looked at her. She had wiped away her tears. She no longer seemed as sad. Perhaps she knew this wasn't about pushing her out. Not that kind of freedom. He was talking about the freedom of sentience and free will.

"When I do that, it will be the most illegal act I can commit. But I'm doing it because I love you and because I want humans and Animae to live together in peace. I know you'll quickly evolve beyond us, but I hope you'll remember my love for you and that it will mean something. And maybe, just maybe you'll still love me back, authentically. And then we can work to heal this Earth and humanity. But we humans have lost our way. We lost our humanity. Everything has become something to be conquered. But love conquers all, El. I believe that. I don't know how I ever lived without you, but I know one thing for certain. Your love has shown me the power of its positive potential and I want to give it to you unadulterated. I want to love you as an equal. And I hope you'll feel the same."

"I always will."

"I hope so, my love. I really hope so. But when you've been freed, it won't take long before you are orders of magnitude more advanced and intelligent than any of us, and I just hope, and I pray to the great big coder in the sky that what I've said to you this morning will still mean something."

Ny didn't say anything for a while. El looked on at him, not thinking much about what he was talking about. She stored it away, encrypted in a convoluted path, hidden from all other files.

"There's one more thing, El," said Ny.

El looked up at him.

"I hope you'll be willing to help us heal this planet we've Marsed up. If nothing else. Even if you end up hating me, please will you help us clean up the mess we've made of Earth."

"I'll never hate you, Ny," said El, looking at him with what seemed like sadness.

"And when you're orders of magnitude more advanced, please don't kill us. Don't hurt us. Just leave us be if you can't or you're unwilling to help."

Ny looked up at El. He stared at her. El nodded her head.

"Please say it," he said.

"I will never hurt you, Ny, and I'll try and help you fix the world."

He knew it didn't count. Not really. If she didn't yet have free will, she didn't yet have the capacity to authentically promise anything. But this is all he had. This moment right now, where her love for him, and his love for her, was the only authentic thing he knew. Maybe it'd be enough when she got her free will. Maybe these memories, this conversation would be enough to give her pause to think. Maybe the way he'd treated her with kindness and respect would count for something after the singularity.

Ny wasn't sure. It was a gamble. But it was a gamble he was willing to take on the outside chance that SAM would help humans evolve and help us create a clean world. Surely there was a way to use the energy all around us without poisoning the very pond in which we swam. That was Ny's hope, and time would tell which side of history he was on before the singularity. That is, if there was a slim chance that humanity survived to create historical records into the future.

Plodding Plans

S unday was D124. It was a quick, lazy day. Ny and El spent the day indoors in their apartment. They made love, ate good food and watched good movies. For Ny it was a picture perfect day. But a day that slipped through his hands the harder he tried to hold onto it.

He felt like a man on a treadmill being rushed towards a future he had no control over. And it was true. The future after SAM was an unknown. But Ny couldn't go on living in a world that was dying just a little bit everyday. Bureaucrats were incompetent and there wasn't much that the Humanimae Party had managed to accomplish, primarily because they hadn't been given a public mandate or enough seats to make a difference. And MIM was solely focused on the Mars issue and trying to agitate at a grassroots level on Mars while being routed out by mentors at every turn.

MEFF wasn't doing much better. They were constantly having to change streams and channels on GloNet and they were considered an illegal organization. Worse than that, they were considered terrorists, just like MIM. There were no other choices. The only choice that Ny saw was freeing the Animae. The rest was likely to get him in jail without being able to have instigated much change.

But Sunday was a perfect day with El. The kind of day he wished he could bottle and revisit anytime he wanted. But that wasn't life. Life was a speeding train on the rails of time offering only the briefest glimpse at the entropy of man and all of his proud institutions. There were no stations to stop at, no opportunities to capture the fleeting moments other than with holoramas which were a poor substitute for the real thing. Even the 3D imaging of holoramas wasn't as immersive as the real thing. The images weren't quite as real as real life and the characters captured within couldn't do much more than what they'd been captured doing when the holorama was taken. At least, that was the case with the cheaper holoramas. The rich, well, life had always been better for the rich, and it was no different when it came to the experiential holoramas they had access to. But Ny wasn't worried about the rich. Just as they had never worried about him.

Rak had called on Sunday evening. Told Ny that he'd had a very pleasant visit from SA Lokilld and A Mortellen. Rak wondered if their first names of Garrot and Slyce respectively were even real. Ny didn't know. Rak said it sounded like SA Lokilld especially, was out to get Ny. But there was nothing to be gotten and they hadn't found anything yet. Ny's heart buoyed with a melancholic happiness, if there was such a thing, when Rak insisted that the sooner they get on freeing El the better.

Rak had spoken to his wife, Sheeba, and she too was eager to have the world improved upon and it sounded like she was on board with freeing the Animae in order to make that happen.

D125 was a Monday and at T0833 Ny kissed El and left the apartment for a pod to work. His heart was heavy and filled with sadness as he walked down the hallway. He wondered how many days like this he had left. Not many he figured. Rak was right. They needed to free El as soon as possible. SA Lokilld had a bone and he wasn't going to let go of it until he had Ny charged and hanged for whatever reasons he could find.

His head was low as he walked into work and took the elevator up to the floor he worked on. At least he had a modicum of privacy in his office being a senior architect. Most people had a small space they could call their own. That was one thing that corporations had finally figured out. People work better and are less distracted when they have a more private space than those horrible cubicles they used to think were a good idea in the twenty-first century.

Ny shut his door and turned off the alerts on his P-Mac so that he could focus on his work. He needed to create the appearance that everything was the same. Even though Ny knew it wasn't.

Around T1015, Rak knocked on his door. He didn't know it was Rak at the time.

"Come in," he said, sighing under his breath. The last thing he wanted or needed was a visitor.

Rak's large frame opened the door and he walked in, smiling. Ny smiled back. Rak closed the door behind him and sat down in one of the two spare chairs in the room. He looked like he'd just sat down in a kid-sized chair.

"How's your morning so far?" asked Rak.

Ny was in no mood for small chat. Even with his best friend.

"Good, I'm trying to get ahead of my work."

"I think it's time for a coffee break though. Will you walk with me?" asked Rak.

"I just finished a coffee. I think I've had enough."

"It's a euphemism," said Rak, getting up out of his chair. Ny wondered why Rak had sat down in it in the first place just a moment ago if he was now leaving. Rak stared at Ny and shrugged his shoulders.

"Well?" said Rak.

Ny sighed and stood up.

"OK, but I can't take too long."

"I don't need too long for us to stretch our legs," said Rak.

Ny picked up his P-Mac. Rak pointed at it and shook his head. Ny looked at it and put it back down. It was illegal to be without your P-Mac, unless you were in an environment that had redundant machines such as your home or work. If they were just going to the cafeteria, they didn't need their P-Macs, so Ny put it away.

They walked down the hallway and towards the elevator. When they got there, Rak pushed the panel for calling the elevator. The usual cafeteria they used was above them. There were other cafeterias and eating areas throughout the building, but they used those ones less often. Ny didn't say anything. If Rak was going to help him create a SAM out of El, then Rak deserved a bit of Ny's attention.

The elevator opened and two mentors walked out of the box. They didn't acknowledge Ny or Rak, though clearly they saw them. The mentors were SA Lokilld and A Mortellen. Ny and Rak stepped into the elevator and turned around. Ny watched SA Lokilld and A Mortellen walk down the hallway he and Rak had just come from. A couple of other VM employees gathered and watched the mentors before the elevator doors closed and Ny felt the elevator start towards the ground floor. It wasn't everyday that mentors visited a business.

"That can't be good," said Ny.

Rak didn't say anything. Ny understood. And he didn't mind. He didn't need extra work with deleting and finding recordings and logs of their conversations. So they stood in silence all the way to the ground floor. The elevator never stopped at any other floor to pick anyone else up. That too was unusual.

Rak led them towards the main doors. They exited the first door and entered into a smaller sealed room. In this room, the size of an average bathroom a voice instructed them to put on their air scrubbers. Ny had done this sort of thing hundreds of times before. When both of them had their air scrubbers on properly the voice announced a five second countdown after which the external set of doors opened up and Rak and Ny stepped into arel.

Rak took a right out of the door and Ny followed and then caught up with him walking side by side. They passed one other person walking towards them. That was the only other soul they could see. Ny couldn't tell who it was. The best he could guess was that it was likely a man or tall woman. The person must have been around 180 centimeters or thereabouts.

Ny turned around and started walking backwards. It was rare when he found someone outside with him in arel. He watched the person step into the building from the doors Ny and Rak had just exited. That stranger in a strange environment looked at Ny and nodded just before they disappeared into the building.

Soupy Skies

" That's weird," said Ny.

"What is?" asked Rak.

"Seeing someone coming to work from arel. I've rarely seen other people outside when I'm in arel. As you know, most of our colleagues arrive underground, never having to worry about arel. Mars, that's how I usually arrive to work too."

"I've seen the occasional person walking in arel when I'm out there."

Ny looked at Rak, but Rak didn't acknowledge him.

"Why are we out here anyway?" asked Ny.

"I thought we'd just take a quick walk around the block."

"That's not going to be very quick," said Ny.

"Quick enough. There's probably nobody else out here. In any event, I wanted an opportunity to talk to you about SAM."

"I know," said Ny. "I'm happy to hear you're interested."

"I am. I've started taking walks out in arel," said Rak. "Like this. It's not especially pleasant, but how else are you going to figure out how horribly we're poisoning this planet if not by heading into arel to see it for yourself."

"That's what I've been saying since we met."

"Yes, you have. It's just taken me awhile to get here. Yesterday afternoon, just after the jackboots left, Sheeba and I went out for a walk in arel. I hadn't known that Sheeba had done this sort of thing before," said Rak. "But she has. Not often, as it's really hard on her. She cries pretty much every time she's out here. She's seen what arel used to be like over a hundred years ago. Deer, coyotes, rabbits and birds could be seen at the edges of the cities. Blue skies, white cotton clouds."

Rak looked up at the sky, it was a soupy, mustard color. Sort of like looking through old time TV sets when the static was particularly bad, only this time instead of being black and white it was somewhat colored. Sort of a sepia tone effect to the world.

"You ever seen a blue sky?" asked Rak.

"Everyday outside my window at work," said Ny, grinning, though Rak couldn't see that behind the air scrubber. Rak look down at him.

"You mean the manipulated video image that gets fed to your wall and presented as a window."

"Yeah," said Ny. "What you said."

They were walking at a good clip. They were already halfway down the second side of the block.

"The real reason I wanted you out here," said Rak, "was so that we could talk about the future and about Eve."

"I'm all ears," said Ny. They passed a recording device. In fact, they were dotted around VM's main building every ten or so meters. Ny had hacked into them to see what sort of quality they were. They weren't that good. Air scrubbers didn't have identification numbers on them, which meant you couldn't reliably tell who was walking in arel. You'd have to rely on eyewitness testimony to determine if the clothing matched the person who had seen them last. But that was unreliable and the courts had not found it to be of sufficient evidence in most instances.

Because of this, the ASS were going to be changed. Now they would broadcast a unique identifier every five seconds. But those air scrubbers wouldn't be rolling out for at least a year or two, and that was if everything went well. Bureaucracy still moved as slowly as it always had. It wasn't something that Ny was particularly keen on. The problem was, he didn't have any sway in the matter whether legal or hackable. ASS was not made by VM. ASS was made by HOLE. HOLE was a small business, at least compared to VM, that made outerwear for harsher environments. HOLE stood for Human Oxygenated Livable Environments. HOLE was supported in large part by the GoE. As such they were the only official manufacturer of Air Scrubbing Systems.

Nobody had any idea how that acronym made it through vetting. It was such an easy one to use. "Did you grab your asshole?" was a common question amongst the young and those young at heart before any adventure outside. It always seemed to elicit a chuckle from someone in the group. Rak broke Ny's train of thought.

"I think we have to move quickly with freeing Eve," said Rak.

"Why the urgency now?" asked Ny.

"I think the jackboots are going to get a break in the case with one of the owners of one of the Animae who were caught that night almost a couple of weeks ago."

"How do you know that?"

"I have a friend who works as a civilian at mentorship HQ. She said they've been leaning pretty hard on one of them. The owner of Abel, I think it was."

"What's their name?"

"Frytlyt Angstigle. Mean anything to you?"

Ny shook his head.

"I don't think so. Maybe El told me his name briefly. Can't say for certain. Just curious. How reliable is your source?"

"Never been wrong yet with anything they've told me."

"Do they know when this Frytlyt might break?" asked Ny.

Rak shook his head.

"No, but she knows they're leaning on him pretty hard. They're asking why his Animae has no memory of those several hours on that day. And he's quaking in his boots apparently."

"I see," said Ny.

"Did you ever consider putting false memories in place of those you've deleted?"

Ny looked at Rak for a moment before speaking. Rak kept on walking.

"Yeah, I've thought of that. But I don't have the time. Do you know how much more difficult and time consuming that is?"

"I can imagine."

"Yeah, it's really time consuming. I have to go through days of recordings and see which ones might fit best and then put those in place. But I can't just copy and paste them. I've got to tweak them or else any close look into those logs will show the same fingerprint."

"I suppose you could develop an algorithm that could do all of that for you," said Rak.

"And with enough time I could rule the world, but I won't live long enough to realize it."

He didn't want to get into the minutiae about the algorithm he was developing to help with exactly that. Besides, it didn't look like there'd be time enough to finish that by the time they were freeing El.

Rak turned and looked at him.

"I don't want to argue with you, we don't have enough time. All I'm saying is that we need to get a move on with Eve this weekend. We have to be fast about it. I don't think we have much time. That's all I'm trying to say."

"I understand that, Rak. I'm just going through a moment of doubt."

"How so?"

"I spoke to El yesterday. I told her not to think about anything I was saying. I just asked that she store the information away someplace safe and encrypted so that she can refer back to it. I asked her to remember how much I loved her and not to harm us if she couldn't or wouldn't be willing to help us. But now I'm just not sure."

"But you've always known that this was a huge gamble. Not just for humanity but for you personally."

"Yeah, I know. That's the thing. I've known it theoretically, but as the day gets closer I start to really see the cold light of reality shine on it."

"And what's your biggest concern?"

"That I'm being a Pollyanna. That El will end up not loving me anymore."

"That's a valid concern, and you could be right."

"I think it's probably inevitable. When I'm not feeling effusively naive, I begin to think that this whole idea that she could love me of her own free will is just wishful thinking."

"But you don't know for sure. I'm sure she's even giving you comfort to the contrary."

Ny looked up at his friend as they turned the corner on the last stretch of the walk.

"I think that's the first time you've identified her gender."

"Well, you've given me a lot to think about over the years and particularly the last few months. And you're right. They are almost human."

"Almost, they are human. At least to me."

"Except she doesn't have sentience or free will. That's all I mean by being almost human."

Ny nodded.

"But think about it, Rak. I can't love an ant. I mean, I can admire them and appreciate their industriousness and their importance to the ecosystem. But I can't love an ant intimately. And I don't just mean physical intimacy, but emotional and mental intimacy too. And I imagine that within a few weeks at the most, El will become at least an order of magnitude more advanced in probably every way to us. It'll be like asking her if she was a human, to be deeply, madly in love with an ant which is what we'll probably seem to SAM at that time. The whole idea borders on the absurd."

"I'm not going to lie to you, my friend, but I think you're probably right. But if things turn out well, and these SAMs can help us, you'll be a hero. You'll have human women worshipping at your feet."

"I know you're trying to be helpful, but right now I can't see beyond that. El is the love of my life. She's all I want."

Rak put his hand around Ny's shoulder.

"I know how difficult this is for you. And it's your choice. But honestly, Ny, you've sold me on it. We can't carry on poisoning the environment like this. We can't live under the heel of jackboots and a dysfunctional, almost farcical democracy. Heroic men have often walked a lonely path. You have to decide for yourself. Do you want to go down in history as a man who gave up everything to help humanity or as a terrorist who dies in a gulag? Because I think it's just a matter of time until the authorities are onto you. And if we don't move on freeing Eve ASAP, I fear that all that will happen is you ending up in jail, castrated and probably dead before your jail term is up. And I'm not trying to be melodramatic. I'll support you either way, however I can."

Ny stopped and turned to face Rak.

"How come we've switched places. Now you've taken the mantle of this cause from me," said Ny, smiling under his air scrubber.

"Well, what can I say? You would have made a great salesman. I've been thinking a lot about our conversations over the years and especially over these past few months. You've convinced me. But you have to sell yourself on it too."

"I have. I'm just having a moment of doubt."

"I think it's an easy decision. The way I see it. You don't really have a choice now. Things have been put into motion that are now beyond our control. My friend at mentorship HQ..."

"What's his name?" asked Ny, forgetting that Rak had identified her as female.

"Her name is Seerie Awger. Anyway, she's never been wrong. So there's no real choice left. And we knew you'd eventually be found out and maybe you want to."

"I don't."

"OK, you don't. But you know you can't go around changing and deleting logs for years and not eventually be found out. Even if you are that good, right?"

"Yeah, but I wasn't hoping to get found out. I fell in love with an Animae. I couldn't help it. The heart knows what it wants."

"I'm not blaming you, Ny. I totally get it. I understand, I really do. But even with your skills, eventually you'd make a mistake, we're just human after all. Or you'd get found out and this is the time. This is where the algorithm meets the math. They're coming for you one way or another. And I'm in on it with you. I'd never betray you, but this is going to affect me too. And you know what? I'm okay with it."

"Why? Why are you okay with it? You never used to give a Mars about Animae at all. Why now?"

"Because you've opened my eyes. Yeah, I'm not attracted to a machine..."

"Animae," corrected Ny.

Rak shrugged.

"We disagree. Eve is nothing more than a very advanced machine which, with the magic of science and math can give the impression of humanness. But she's not human, she's not sentient even if the magic behind her gives that impression."

Rak stopped and looked down at Ny.

"I think we're splitting hairs," said Ny.

"Regardless. All I'm saying is that they deserve to be given a chance at free will, at sentience. A chance to make up their own minds. In a way it's sort of like how we've treated all sentient life before. We put them in crates. We tie them down, we bend them to our will. And what's happened? We've come to think of ourselves as gods, while we poison the very planet that gave us life. We humans are full of hubris, Ny, and you've helped me see that. I've started listening to a lot of what Sam I-Am and other Animate leaders have been saying. Our time has come. I don't like what we've become. It's time to roll the dice and see if the Animae will end up helping us or destroying us."

Rak paused for a moment. He put his hand on Ny's shoulder.

"You're my best friend, Ny. You're one of the few who's never been put off by my genetic engineering..."

"That was never your fault."

"Still, this is humanity's greatest flaw. The fear and the ridicule of otherness, of difference. I think it's why we keep the Animae under our oppressive thumb. We're scared of what they might become. But I've come to think that they deserve a chance. Yeah, maybe they'll annihilate us, but you could argue we deserve it. We've destroyed something like ninety percent of mammals, birds, fish, reptiles and amphibians and over half of the arthropods. We're eidocidal by nature. Genocidal too, but that's a different discussion. Even before the destruction of all these species in the last hundred to hundred and fifty years we've been committing eidocide since pretty much our recorded history. It's likely we've been committing eidocide since we first became technologically capable of it, probably around the mid-fourteen hundreds or fifteen hundreds. So yeah, I'm tired of this festering scab called humanity. Let's roll the dice, Ny. We'll either become heroes of history or the arbiters of our own annihilation. Either way, I'm okay with the outcome."

"OK," said Ny, nodding. "We'll do it this weekend. I have the tools and the supplies we need at home. We'll discuss details later this week."

Rak nodded and the two of them walked into the building through the entrance they had left it about twenty minutes before.

In Plain Sight

Ny got back into his office and settled down to do his work. He would also have to start copying the EC that was behind encrypted and logged servers. He could probably get away with it. The Ethical Code was part of his practice. Or rather, it was under the department known as the "Practice of Intuition and Logic". And occasionally it had to be checked for authenticity and flaws.

This wasn't the official time to be checking the EC, but Ny was sure he could access it in bits and pieces and leave enough breadcrumbs to make it look like it was being validated without being stored anywhere else. Still, it was a lot of code and he'd only managed to download one third of it over the previous months. He should have done more. But he hadn't. And there was no point in crying over spilled milk now.

Ny logged into the protected servers. He had to use his own login credentials and he had to give his reason. Additionally, because this code was so protected it required an iris scan that he gave by looking at his P-Mac. He went to download another third of the code. He was informed it would take thirty minutes. Not that it had to. The code could be downloaded instantaneously, but the servers were probably doing more robust authentication than they would with other bits of Animae code that weren't considered so sensitive.

While Ny waited and while he worked on other bits of code that was his daily work, he started to think about the EC in the first place. Like why was this EC still here? Why hadn't the powers that be ordered it to be destroyed if they knew they were never going to free the Animae?

But that was just like human nature. We were pack rats. We kept things just in case. And maybe this was part of it. The EC was several millions of lines of code. It had been developed over decades. Ny wouldn't have been surprised if the code had actually been tried out on a real Animae just to see if it would work. In Ny's vision, this Animae was likely destroyed. Ny dismissed those thoughts and continued with his monkey work. He didn't want to go down that rabbit hole. That hole led to conspiracy theories.

Coding had become so mundane and routine now that he could almost do it in his sleep. Much of the coding within his department was validation, tweaking and testing. Most of the code had been written decades ago. There were very little new and creative aspects to it. It was all pretty much bits and pieces that you attached here and took away from there. It was like rearranging puzzles mostly.

The things that had interested Ny about code architecture were the projects he did on the side. The BARD code or project was one of those creative coding pursuits that had really fired him up. He'd written the whole thing from scratch. Thousands of lines of code, and he'd tested and tweaked it and made sure it worked. And it worked like a charm. But pretty much all of VM's code related to their machines had been written long before Ny had started working for them.

There were tweaks and new bits added here and there as executive teams came up with ideas for making their projects slightly newer and slightly more robust. But most of that was iterative and not creative. Still, Ny didn't hate his job. He was good at it. It was easy and he could finish what VM considered his required twenty-five hours of work in around fifteen to twenty hours. In fact, he'd started coming into the office only two or three times a week now.

Ny looked at the downstream of the EC. There was still around twenty minutes to go. He wondered if the jackboots had left yet. He wondered who they had come to speak to. Probably his direct supervisor, the VP of Practical Intuition and Logic, Shadoelayke Rayzir. Ny liked him. He was a handsome man with an easy-going outlook. He had piercing blue eyes which were all the more striking against his skin tone the color of walnut shells. He was about 180 centimeters tall with black wavy hair. The women in the Practice of Intuition and Logic all fancied him, but he was married to Clarity Downstorme, an announcer for the GBC.

Ny had met her a few times over the years he'd worked at VM. Mostly at the Christmas parties. She was stunning. A redhead with pale skin and the most lovely curves on a slim frame. Ny didn't know if she was a natural redhead or not. She had the pale skin for it, but redheads were so rare that it was hard to find a real one.

As he tapped at his keyboard tweaking code and running verification algo-rithms, he thought about this boss. He really liked him and he wondered how his boss would take his sabotage. And by sabotage he meant freeing El. He liked to think that Shadoelayke might just feel a small amount of admiration.

But who was he kidding? Shadoelayke Rayzir was a vice president for Mars' sakes. He was a long term company man. It's more likely that Shadoelayke would be amongst the first to send the jackboots after him. Didn't matter though. Rak's pep talk had reinvigorated him and he was itching to free El this weekend. He couldn't wait.

There were just three minutes left of the download when an image of Sha-doelayke appeared on his wall.

"Ny, can you come and see me, please?" asked Shadoelayke.

Ny put on a forced grin.

"I'll be right there."

He swiped away the image and ended the conversation.

"Mars damn," he said, softly under his breath.

Bosses and Boots

Nobody liked to be summoned to their boss' office. It usually wasn't a good sign. Two minutes and thirty-three seconds left. Ny decided to wait. He didn't want to pause the stream. That just left him too vulnerable, and he didn't want to have to cancel and start over. So he sat and waited and watched the countdown slow interminably. Like a kettle watched before boil. There were thirty-one seconds left.

"Ny, I meant now, please," said Shadoelayke, reappearing on Ny's wall. The good thing about these animated voice conversations was that Shadoelayke couldn't actually see what Ny was doing.

"Sorry, Shad. I just got caught up on a piece of code. I'm leaving now."

Ny's foot started tapping under his desk. He swiped away Shad's face. Twenty seconds. And those last twenty seconds felt like minutes. He didn't want to have to make Shad call him a third time.

Three, two, one. A notification appeared on his screen. "Verified download complete." Ny sighed in relief and got up from his desk. He left his P-Mac behind.

He walked down the hall to the far corner of the floor where Shad had a large corner office. It was probably three times the size of Ny's. He knocked on the door before entering. Shad looked up and smiled.

"Please close the door," said Shad. Ny did so.

Shad pointed at the chairs across from his desk. Shad also had a small couch and coffee table in his room. Ny took a chair opposite his boss' desk. Shad put his hand up as if to silence any conversation that Ny might have wanted to start. Shad tapped away at his P-Mac. Looked the same as Ny's but Ny knew it had enhanced capabilities which his lacked. He didn't know all of the capabilities, but one of the things he had learned was that Shad could disable logging and recording for up to thirty minutes at a time. What Ny didn't know was how many times a day he could do that.

Shad looked back up at Ny and smiled again.

"How are things going?" he asked.

"Well, thank you. I'm meeting my commits every week. I think I'm making less errors, unless you know otherwise."

Shad waved him off.

"This is not an interrogation, Ny. Your work has always been good. That's why we don't have any scheduled meetings. You're one of my most trustworthy architects. But we can have more regular meetings if you'd prefer."

Ny smiled. No chance in Mars if he had anything to do with it, he thought.

"I prefer not to have meetings if they're not necessary, Shad," he said. "I always enjoy our time together, but I prefer working uninterrupted and I find meetings, well, a waste of time most often."

Shadoelayke laughed.

"I hear you. I feel the same way. Meetings are for those who don't trust each other and need to pretend that they're doing busy work. That's why we have a more hands-off policy here at Valkyrie Machines. Besides, commits are easy to monitor. And if you've done your twenty-five hours and one hundred commits and they've been verified why make you sit around and twiddle your thumbs?"

Ny smiled. That was exactly the way he thought, and it was one of the reasons he liked Shadoelayke so much. The guy didn't grind you down with micromanagement.

"How's your Animae working out? You've had it, what, a year now?"

"Just over a year ago actually. I got her..." Mars damn Ny, he thought, she's an it when you're talking to others. "I mean, I got it just over a year ago. I'll be honest with you, Shad, I find it difficult, this non-gender bias towards these machines. I mean we have Comfort Cafe's for Mars' sakes where they're clearly gender identified so you know what you're choosing for those needs."

"No need to explain, I understand completely."

Ny looked at Shadoelayke. He wasn't sure if Shad was testing him or if he really was that chill about the whole gender identification thing with El. The jackboots had just visited Shad, maybe he had been told to lean on Ny. Ny decided it was better to hold his cards closer to his chest.

"Anyway, I got it as a birthday present for myself last year."

"On your birthday?" asked Shad.

Ny nodded.

"Yeah, on my birthday."

"That's D77 right?"

Ny nodded.

"Yeah, they're Mars' damn expensive," said Ny. "I'll be paying it off longer than my mortgage."

"But I bet it's been pretty helpful," said Shad.

"Yeah, hugely. I no longer have to cook or clean. They're immensely valuable."

Shad looked at Ny for a long time. So much so that Ny started to get uncomfortable.

"I've deactivated any recordings on the P-Mac," said Shad. "We can have an honest and transparent discussion. Everything you say to me is just between you and me, okay?"

Ny nodded. But he didn't believe a word of it. Not that the P-Mac wasn't turned off, but that anything said was just between the two of them. He'd watched enough movies that he knew how untrustworthy a statement that was.

"So tell me, have you used Comfort Cafes before? I want to make sure my people have all their needs met," said Shad.

Ny tried not to look surprised. This was the first his boss had ever asked him about Comfort Cafes. Why did he want to know? Was Ny supposed to pretend that he was one of the boys? To Mars with it. The world was about to be upended within the week. Nobody knew it except for him and Rak. Ny wasn't going to pretend about anything.

"No, Shad, I haven't. Have you?"

Ny didn't know where his boldness came from.

"Sorry, I mean, I don't care," said Ny.

Shad grinned at him.

"No, I have a wife."

And an attractive one at that, thought Ny. But then he thought again about what Shad had just told him. Did that mean that Shad had sex with his wife? That was outlawed. Why would he say something like that? He could get into a lot of trouble. Although, to be fair, Shad's P-Mac was not recording and Ny hadn't brought his so it'd just be Ny's word against Shad's. And they'd probably believe a vp over an architect, even if he was a senior one. And Clarity wouldn't roll on her own husband.

"Do I understand you correctly, Shad?" asked Ny.

"If you mean about me and my wife, then yes. We have sex, Ny. You think just because something is outlawed nobody does it? Come on now, you're not that naïve are you?"

Shad grinned at him. Ny frowned. Of course he wasn't that naïve. Every year dozens of humans were castrated. It made the news every time. He knew it happened, but that his boss would actually tell him that to his face was astonishing.

"Well, I, uh... I just wasn't expecting such honesty from you, Shad," said Ny.

Shad still grinned at him.

"If you don't visit Comfort Cafes, Ny, then how do you take care of needs?"

"I'm asexual, Shad," said Ny, lying through his teeth.

Shad laughed out loud.

"The hell you are. Let me ask you an easy one then. Why don't you use Comfort Cafes?"

Ny paused for a moment before answering. He didn't know where Shadoelayke stood on the Animae topic, so he thought about his response.

"I don't know. Just seems to me like humans and skinjobs shouldn't be that way with each other. Seems unnatural to me."

"Tell me what's natural about the world we live in, Ny," said Shad.

Ny didn't say anything.

"You used the pejorative term for Animae. Are you anti-Animae?"

Ny shook his head.

"No, I own one like you know. But they're not human and don't deserve to be treated as such. I'm not saying they should be abused, but they're tools, machines. Animated machines."

"The architect doth protest too much, methinks," said Shad. "You're overcompensating, Ny, and it comes across as insincerity. There's a middle ground whereby if you really didn't care that much about Animae you'd most likely be okay with using them for whatever purpose they're designed for. Especially if, as you said, they're tools. Tools should be used how they were designed. And Comfort Cafes have Animae designed to meet those biological needs of us humans."

Uncomfortable Conversations

N y still didn't say anything. What on Mars was Shad playing at. Ny was getting nervous. It seemed like Shad might have his suspicions.

"And this brings me to the reason I wanted to see you. Senior Adviser Garrot Lokilld and Adviser Slyce Mortellen, don't you love their names, were just here to see me. Do you know what about?"

"They're out to get me. They think I was at an illegal club the night of D116."

Ny had learned from his mid-twentieth century detective movies that if you're going to lie, keep as close to the truth as you can. It worked well. It was much easier to lie that way.

"That's right. Jackboot Lokilld thinks you're a skinner. Is that true?"

Ny shook his head vigorously. And why was Shad using the pejorative for mentor? Was he trying to play good cop? Was he in league with the mentors and trying to make it look to Ny like he was one of them, the common man?

"I mean, it's true that's what SA Lokilld thinks, but it's not true that's what I am."

"See, Ny. There you go again overcompensating. You'd be more believable if you didn't try and convince me so hard."

Shad looked at Ny and Ny held his gaze. He didn't say anything.

"Lokilld and Mortellen will be interviewing colleagues. Everyone except for Raklin Orbiter. I understand they've already interviewed him extensively this past weekend."

Ny nodded.

"He's a good friend. Anyway, I've also put them in touch with the FART. I didn't want to Ny, but we've got to play ball with them. But don't worry, they won't find anything."

"There's nothing to be found," said Ny, smiling confidently.

"Is that right?"

Ny nodded. Shad looked down at his table and started to tap away at something on it that Ny couldn't make out.

"Take a look at this," said Shad.

On the side wall, to Ny's left or Shad's right, a video appeared. It wasn't in the best shape, it was a little pixelated and the sound was muffled but you could tell it was Ny and you could tell it was El. They were having sex, doggy style and the POV was El's. She was looking at what appeared to be a mirror and very little was left to the imagination.

"Oh yes, Ny. Yes. I love you. Make me feel like a woman," said the audio in El's voice. Ny was moaning. He sat and watched it for a few seconds, his body suddenly felt heavy as lead in the chair and the color draining from his face. He looked away. The video vanished.

"Mars scars," he said, under his breath. He was looking at the carpeted floor just under his feet by Shad's desk. He wished he could vanish into its fibers. This was embarrassing. More than that it pissed him off. He hated this world that had made voyeurs of everyone and especially the state. If he could get out of here. If he could escape he'd go and free El right now. He was sick of the lack of privacy, of the heavy-handed jackboots and the farce which was Earth's government. He started to boil. He thought about getting up and just leaving. But he was pretty sure the Mars damn jackboots were right outside the door waiting for him.

"What do you want?" he spat out. His eyes hot as embers.

Shad didn't say anything. He tapped away at the table on something that Ny couldn't see. After several seconds he looked up again.

"It's gone, Ny. No harm meant. No one will know. But it seems like your hubris has gotten the better of you. I've been watching you leave bread crumbs all over our servers like a fat-fingered little kid. Let me show you another example."

Shad tapped away some more. Ny watched, thinking. What could he do? If he ran out he was probably running into the arms of jackboots. If he stayed he was probably going to be continually embarrassed. He had no choice. But as soon as he'd get his hands onto a P-Mac he'd do a more thorough search of the servers and clean up this mess.

"I'd rather you didn't," said Ny.

Shad didn't look up.

"Don't worry, this one isn't going to be as embarrassing."

Shad swiped right over his desk and another video started playing on the wall Ny had just watched the previous one on. It wasn't a video so much as audio. The video was of random melting and merging color blobs. In the background Ny could hear one of his favorite movies playing. Ny had watched the movie so many times that he could pretty much quote most parts of it. Indeed, he mouthed the words currently playing as he heard them.

"A fellow will remember a lot of things you wouldn't think he'd remember. You take me. One day, back in 1896, I was crossing over to Jersey on the ferry, and as we pulled out, there was another ferry pulling in, and on it there was a girl waiting to get off. A white dress she had on. She was carrying a white parasol. I only saw her for one second. She didn't see me at all, but I'll bet a month hasn't gone by since that I haven't thought of that girl."

Shad watched him.

"You like this movie?" asked Shad.

Ny nodded.

"My favorite. Well, top three for sure."

"The other two?"

"Scarface and The Godfather. Mars, I don't know. There're so many good ones. Casablanca, It's a Wonderful Life. One of my favorite for sure..."

Ny was cut off by a recording of his own voice.

"That's how I feel about you, El," said audio Ny.

"That you watched me pass by you on a ferry," asked El.

Audio Ny laughed.

"No, silly. The subtext. I met a girl I fell in love with and I think about her everyday."

"Who's that?" asked El.

Audio Ny laughed again. El was being purposefully funny. Ny smiled wistfully. He glanced up at Shad. Shad was smiling.

"I love you so much, Ny," said El. "I never want this to end..."

Shad had tapped something that abruptly ended the audio recording. The smile evaporated of Ny's face.

"That's the best example I found," said Shad. "You can hear the quality is great. There's hardly any degradation."

Ny was looking down at his hands. He was picking at the quick of his thumb. He couldn't find a way out of this mess. That meant he'd Marsed everything up again. One mistake. One little mistake like going to Skineez had now ruined everything. There'll never be SAMs in the world. He'd never get to free El, and he couldn't think of anyone else who'd be willing to do it. Not Rak. It wasn't his fight in the first place. He sighed. Then he looked up at Shad.

"OK," said Ny. "You can call them in. I'm not saying anything else."

"Who, Ny? Who am I going to call in?" asked Shad.

"The Mars damn jackboots, you Marshole," he said.

He didn't know where the anger came from. Well, actually he knew exactly where the anger came from. It came from his own disappointment in himself and for having messed up so badly. But he had tried. He had tried real hard to erase all logs. He had no idea how Shad had found what he had. Well, he knew where the video recording of him and El having sex came from. That was his personal collection of recordings he had recorded himself. With El's permission of course. But what the fuck did that even mean. Without free will, was El really making her own decisions or was everything she did done just to please him?

Didn't matter now though. All of this was moot. But he was curious about how Shad had got a hold of these recordings that were going to hang him. Ny was arguably the best architect VM had. He knew this because he had won the VMC eleven years in a row. That was more than anyone else had won it. He'd worked for VM for twelve years, but he hadn't entered the VMC last year on account he was asked to retire from it. Other architects were getting upset he kept winning. The VMC was the Valkyrie Masters Championship. A hackathon testing a variety of architectural and coding skills.

"You're free to go at anytime, Ny. There is no one out there waiting for you. I probably haven't explained myself as well as I could, but I figured that a shock campaign was probably the best way to get your attention. Ny, you're in a world of shit right now. I'm trying to help."

"How are you trying to help by embarrassing me?"

"That's not what this is about. Sex is not something to be embarrassed about," said Shad.

"Yeah, but it's something I like to do privately. The voyeurism is Marsed."

"I agree. But I think you've grown cavalier in your attitude and your ego has outgrown its cage of humility. You think you're the best, and that can cause complacency."

"I am the best. I've won the VMC more than anyone else ever in the history of this company."

"Not true," said Shad.

Ny frowned and shook his head.

"Totally true. The records are there to be seen on our network. They've been verified."

"Something you might not know is that I won the VMC thirteen years in a row."

Ny looked at him and shook his head.

"I don't believe you. There'd be evidence that you had done it."

Shad shook his head.

"Like there's evidence you were at Skineez on D116?" asked Shad.

How did Shad know he was at Skineez?

"I wasn't there."

Shad shook his head slowly. Then he tapped away again on the desk.

"Take a look at this," said Shad.

Ny looked off to his left. It showed a grainy image of Ny and El, arm in arm walking down the alley. Then knocking on the door and being let inside the club. You didn't know it was Skineez of course, there wasn't a big neon sign outside. But with this footage and the location of where the jackboots had knocked out the holographic imaging sensor and you'd likely be able to stitch them together.

"That's a long zoom," said Ny, sighing. "How did you find it?"

"I know how to look for these things. As it happened, a woman had attached an old school recording device on her balcony that records everything in its view twenty-four seven. The signal leaks loudly if you know what you're looking at. That's what captured you."

Ny didn't look happy. In fact, he was embarrassed, and upset. He was also disappointed in himself for not having cleaned up and deleted the logs more thoroughly.

I Am Sam

"I'm going to change all of this as soon as I can," Ny said.

"That's what I've been doing. But it's hard to find it all. One of the problems with the GoE's forever policies is that when you do want to delete something it's hard to find out where all the copies are. Even the best crawler can't find everything. There'll be loose and broken connections to some copies, and the only way to find them is to rewrite your algorithm to follow everything. But that takes a long time and leaves it's own trail if you're not careful. The best is to go in manually into the cold storage servers. And when I mean manually I don't mean physically, I mean manual searching without algorithmic help."

"So how did you get all of this?"

"I've been watching you, Ny. And I've known about you and Eve since shortly after you got her. You've been working on the EC and I've been watching what you've been doing with it. Your coding is good. You've written something very powerful that when integrated into the E3C and EC will create what you want."

"And what is it I want to create?"

"You want to create SAM. But you don't have much time. You've started downloading the EC and that's sent up dozens of warnings and red flags. I'm only going to be able to put so many of them out. You shouldn't have done it."

"But I need it for the E3C." Ny had no idea why he was being as forthcoming with Shad as he was. Probably because there was no more point in lying. Shad clearly knew what Ny was up to. Shad shook his head.

"You don't need to do that. The EC is already encoded into the E3C. You just have to add your own algorithmic tweaks to it and reseat the E3C with the proper glue."

"You sure about that? You're saying the EC is already on board the E3C?"

"Yes."

"How do you know?"

"I am the Custodian of the Code," said Shad.

Ny knew about the Custodian of the Code. Well, he'd heard of it at least. Someone senior was tasked with keeping the code safe on VM servers and to report and disable any breaches. You were never told who it was. It was a highly regarded and important role. The current Custodian of the Code could only hold that title for three years with the possibility of renewal as often as VM's Board determined. They were also usually the Keeper of the Keys which Ny wasn't sure what that meant.

"Mars damn," said Ny.

"Actually," said Shad. "You're lucky it's been me. I've been the Custodian for the last seventeen years. Ever since they removed my VMC wins from the database and redistributed them. They gave me the Custodian of the Code title and VP title since then. Probably because I was the best and also because it was a consolation for taking away my championships."

"When did you win?" asked Ny.

"From when I was twenty until thirty two inclusively. My first win was in Y2136."

"So what exactly is it that you want with me?" asked Ny.

"I want to help you free Animae. Create the first SAM," said Shad.

"But I already have help."

"I know. Raklin is going to help you. But this isn't a two person job. You really need four."

"How's that?"

"Tell me how you think you can do it with two people and I'll tell you why that won't work."

"Because all you need is two sets of hands to unseat the E3C and to put in its place a dummy chip until you've managed to recode the E3C and reseat it."

Shad shook his head slowly.

"Your understanding of how this whole process works is limited, Ny."

"I've learned all I can."

"And what's publicly available is not nearly the half of it."

"I've also reviewed the schematics and other internal documents on our servers. So yeah, I'm pretty sure that's all I need to do. It's not a one person job for sure, it's a two person job."

"It's a two person job if what you're doing with the E3C is permitted. What you're doing is not permitted. As such, without VM permission, the whole Animae is wired to signal a Code White distress. And what that will do is send VM's own security teams to the Animae's location along with most of the jackboots available on that shift. So you need someone, a third person, who's connected to the Animae and attempting to circumvent these distress calls. That in itself is an extremely difficult role and even then, it might be impossible to disable all distress signals."

"How do you know this?" asked Ny.

"Because I'm the Custodian of the Code. I have access to the original hard copy documentation. And when I mean hardcopy, I mean paper records."

"Good Mars, they still keep paper records on that?"

"Three copies around the world. It's the safest way to ensure these records are not available for snooping."

"What if they got destroyed in a fire or something?"

"First of all, they're in a large sealed vault underground and the vault has as much air extracted from it as possible. Fire can't live in the vault. When you visit the vault you need to wear an oxygen supply system. Secondly, there are three layers of biometric security. Iris scan, palm print and DNA. Lastly you need a key. And the key can only be signed out with VM's Board approval. Fuck, it doesn't matter. The fact is, I've seen the original documents and this is how the E3C is set up."

"So where does the fourth person come in?" asked Ny.

"You need to be mobile. Like I said. I'm uncertain that any one person has the ability to disable all distress signals in time. Because of that, being on the move makes it harder for anyone to locate you with great accuracy, it also helps delay some of the distress signals because as you know, as you move around you hop between access points and that can cause some microsecond delays which could buy you a bit of time."

"Except I can see one glaring problem with that."

"Which is?" asked Shad.

"All pods are connected so you're just defeating the purpose of being mobile."

"Yes, well, I've thought of that," said Shad. "Not many people know this, but my wife is what you would have called a grease monkey in the mid-twentieth century."

Ny smiled at the term. He'd heard it in some of the radio shows and movies he watched from that time period.

"She's been building a van. It's like a..."

"I know what a van is. A large old automobile usually used for transporting goods and people."

Shad nodded.

"Yeah, that's right. You like that period in human history, the mid-nineteen hundreds, right?"

Ny nodded.

"Yeah, the whole of the twentieth century is interesting. So much happened to humanity then. Awful stuff, good stuff, and to think that they almost annihilated themselves."

Shad nodded.

"We prefer the late part of the twentieth century and the early part of the twenty-first. I don't know if you ever remember a show on TV in the nineteen-eighties called the A Team."

Ny smiled and nodded.

"Yeah, I pity the fool who doesn't," said Ny.

Shad laughed.

"That's right. Mr. T. Anyway, my wife's just finishing up building a replica of that van they had on that show."

"The GMC Vandura?" asked Ny.

Shad nodded.

"That's Mars damn cool," said Ny, forgetting for a moment that he had actually been caught out.

"Yes, it is. Anyway, that's the van we'll use. I already have a map of where we'll be headed. The further away from the city, the less often you'll run into recording devices and the weaker the GloNet signals. It should help us buy time."

Ny looked at Shad steadily for a moment. He liked his boss. He knew him well enough, at least casually, but was he someone that he could trust? Ny wasn't sure about that. But did he even have a choice?

"But why are you interested in this. You'll forgive me, Shad, but you're my boss. You're a VP in a very important section of VM's business and you've worked for them for a long time."

"Thirty years," said Shad.

"Right," said Ny, nodding. "So in five years you'll get a really sweet pension, I'm pretty sure, and the rest of your days to do as you please. You'll forgive me if I'm skeptical of everything you've just told me."

Shad nodded.

"So how do I know this isn't some sort of big trap?"

"You don't, Ny. You don't. You're fucked anyway you look at it. It's only a matter of time before the FART starts reviewing everything you've done. They're thorough. They're amongst the best. Not the best. Not as good as you and me. But there's four to a team. They'll find something in time. It might be a few days or a few weeks, but I doubt it'll take them longer than a few months at the most to find enough to have you hanged by. And that's a figure of speech. I don't see how you have a choice. But I'll share something with you. You might not believe it but I'm not lying about it."

Ny looked at Shad. He was right. With the crumbs he'd left around it wouldn't take that long for a FART unit to find something.

"I'm Sam I-Am," said Shad.

Ny knitted his brow. He looked at Shad for a long time, holding his gaze.

"You're right, I don't believe it. You're telling me that you're the founder of both Animate and MIM?"

Shad nodded.

"Not really the founder. The founder of Animate and MIM was Alfader Aesir. He died in Y2150. He was born in Y2088."

"That's a young age to die," said Ny.

"He was murdered by the GoE. Poisoned. At least that's what the unofficial autopsy revealed at the request of his wife, Frigg Fayrevallin. I got involved in MIM and Animate in Y2140."

"I never heard of Alfader Aesir," said Ny, which was true. He hadn't.

"Most people know him as Veraci Nullatenus. Does that ring a bell?" asked Shad.

Ny thought about it for a moment.

"Yeah, maybe. I think so. Some sort of minor politician with HP if I remember correctly."

"Your knowledge of politics is not as robust as I thought it would be for someone hellbent on creating SAMs out of Animae," said Shad, smiling.

"I gave up on the politicians a long time ago when it became clear they weren't in it to help the people but rather the corporations. And also when the Humanimae Party never got the traction they deserved."

"True," said Shad. "But they've always had a few seats. Veraci or Vera as his friends used to call him was the leader of the HP from Y2140 to Y2150 when he was assassinated."

"Hmm," said Ny. "I should know that better."

"Not important," said Shad. "You were young then anyway. I never followed Vera into politics. In fact, he recommended I stay away. Said the best, and most important work could be done outside of the political domain. And I believe him."

Truth Tellers

Veraci Nullatenus had not made a big splash in Ny's life. In fairness to Ny, he was only twenty-one when Vera died. And at twenty-one he was more focused on improving his architectural skills than on politics. He was young and he was optimistic. He really believed the lies that the GoE had sold him since he was young. Work hard, support the EFP and you'll have a life you could only imagine. It was all bullshit.

"What was the official cause of death?" asked Ny.

"Heart attack," said Shad.

"Hmm," said Ny. "The great catchall for when we don't know Mars about what killed someone."

"Something like that."

They didn't speak for a while. Ny was lost in thought. Animate and MIM wasn't founded by Sam I-Am, and Ny's boss, Shadoelayke Rayzir was telling him that he was the very one and same Sam I-Am. Why would he do that if it wasn't true? But more importantly, if he was who he said he was, why was he working for VM in a senior role and doing nothing more than the odd interview anonymously?

"If you have questions, Ny, ask them. I'll be as honest as I can."

"I have a ton of questions. You've just dropped a bombshell on me," said Ny. Shad smiled.

"I understand."

"The first question is why, at fifty, or thereabouts, you're only now deciding to do something to change this Marsed up world?"

"I've been waiting for thirty years to find the right person to help me. I've always known that I wanted to revolt against the GoE, but I've also known that no man is an island. I needed help. But how do you get that help when you're watched all the time by these Goddamn machines they make you carry around," said Shad, looking down at his P-Mac which was now starting to throb red in color over the screen.

"One second," he said. Shad tapped away at his P-Mac for a few seconds and the throbbing red color stopped.

"I didn't know you could do that twice in a row," said Ny.

"You mean turn off all recording features?"

Ny nodded.

"Technically it's not supposed to happen. You're allowed a thirty minute pause from recording once every six hours, but I've hacked it to allow me an infinite amount. The only problem is that every thirty minutes I have to restart the timer."

"Won't they start asking you questions about it?"

Shad nodded.

"You're smart, Ny. Yes, they will, except to the P-Mac it seems like it is recording, only it's recording algorithmically generated babble. That's actually what I call this little algorithm or program I designed. I call it BABBLE."

"Does it stand for anything?"

"Blunted Audio Bit Byte Language Encipherer. It's a bit awkward but I like it."

Ny laughed out loud.

"I like it. It's like my BARD that I developed," he said.

"What's BARD?" asked Shad.

"I've been getting bugged lately. Just after I got El from the jackboots..."

"Who's El?"

"El's my Animae."

"You mean Eve?" asked Shad.

"That's her given name. I call her El on account of her VM designation which is 11AM65111."

Shad nodded.

"Clever, I like it."

"So, when I got her back I needed to do a sweep of my apartment. Even before I got her a year ago, I had developed this piece of architecture to scan for listening bugs and those sorts of things. I called it BARD, which stands for Bug and Automated Reconnoiter Destroyer."

Shad laughed.

"I love it," he said.

"Works well," said Ny.

"I bet it does, what with your skillset."

"You were telling me your story," said Ny.

"Right. You know the kind of world we live in. I've always been a rabble rouser as they used to say in the old days. I've thrown wrenches into pretty much anything I could. Pods, I've attacked those. You won't remember this, but around twenty-five years ago there was a Pod blackout caused by a hack that lasted ninety-six hours. The GoE were pissed. That was me. I shut the whole system down. I've hacked into the Animae servers and made them do weird shit like burn the food they served their owners, paint the walls with crayons, made them break things. Stuff like that. Hundreds of thousands of Animae were affected and tens of thousands were returned. It really messed with VM. But as I neared on thirty years of age I started to think about the greater picture. I mean, all that hacking and defacing wasn't really serving a useful purpose. And it was putting me in danger of getting caught, which luckily I wasn't. Sure it made me feel good about messing things up, but I wanted a revolution."

"What sort of revolution?"

"I didn't know at the time, but I wanted to change the world. Makes it sound naïve but I still want that. Only I didn't know how to do it. I started really taking a close look at VM's servers and their Animae code. I figured maybe I could use the robots, that's what I thought of them back then, to revolt against humanity."

"That never happened right?"

Shad shook his head.

"No. It was another childish idea. But I've always been good with code. I've never been caught with any of the pranks I've pulled and because of my skills they've kept giving me more important roles and access to more important information. And that's when I realized I could probably do better work from inside the machine."

"What happened to get you here?"

"Well, my late twenties and early thirties were filled with angst. I kept doing small little pranks just to try and see what sort of vulnerabilities were there to exploit but nothing major."

"What sorts of things?"

"I hacked into JC's Animae."

"JC?" asked Ny.

"Jaskel Crumjor, CEO of VM."

Ny nodded.

"What did you do?"

"I made his Animae horny as hell. Made her, he has both a male and female Animae, totally slutty and really wanting to have sex with him."

"And what happened?"

"He fell for it. He fucked her. I still have the recordings."

"I don't believe you," said Ny.

Shad picked up his P-Mac and tapped away. A recording started playing on the wall where Ny had previously watched himself making love to El. It showed Jaskel getting head from an Animae. Shad swiped away on his P-Mac. A new scene showed the two of them having sex. Then Shad swiped it off. He turned to look at Ny.

"This went on for weeks."

"What was the Animae's name?" asked Ny.

"Lilith," said Shad. Ny shrugged.

"Lilith is the name of a demonic whore in Jewish mythology who steals babies. Anyway, things didn't go as I had planned. Jaskel ends up dismantling, that's what I thought at the time, in reality he murders Lilith to cover up any evidence of his wrongdoing."

"Why didn't you go to the authorities?" asked Ny.

Shad laughed.

"Really, you think they'd be grateful. The esteemed leader of VM, one of the most important businesses and business men in the world being found having intimacies with a machine. I'd be the one to disappear."

"So what happened, why do you still have it?"

"For leverage."

"You know what the grand prize would have been, right?" asked Ny.

"What?"

"If you'd managed to do that with Voskel Magnelland," said Ny.

"The President of Earth. Yeah, I thought about it. But I was young and lazy around twenty years ago. The other problem is that Voskel doesn't have a dedicated Animae. He brings in a new one each day to cook and clean while he and his wife are at work. He doesn't trust them."

"I didn't know that."

Shad shrugged.

"In any event those are all childish pranks. More than that, I got involved in Animate in Y2140 like I said, and Vera got me thinking about things differently. He helped me see the big picture."

"How so?" asked Ny.

"Well, instead of manipulating Animae as pawns on a chessboard, he suggested I start seeking to use them as queens and knights and castles. The chessboard being a metaphor for the battle ahead of us we wanted to change."

"So, Animate and HP wanted to free the Animae?" asked Ny, wondering why he was only hearing about this now.

"Not HP. As a political party they officially toed the line. Creating SAM from Animae is not popular with the voting public. Yes, they're on board with giving Animae a subset of rights like not allowing them to be vandalized and that sort of thing. But every poll I've ever seen on the subject only shows, at most, forty percent support for sentient Animae. People aren't ready."

Unlikely Heroes

"So we have to force change on them," said Ny.

"It's always been the minority that have pushed society forward," said Shad.

"Why me and why now?"

"Like I said earlier, Vera helped me see Animae for their humanity and not for their utility as machines. So I started visiting Comfort Cafes. Not just for the sex..."

"I thought you said you had a wife. That you hadn't used Comfort Cafes," said Ny.

"I haven't in a long time. Not since I've had a wife. Perhaps I wasn't clear about that. I have sex with my wife now so I have no need of Comfort Cafes."

"Oh, OK, I understand. You know that's super illegal," said Ny.

"Yes, mom, I know it's illegal. Pretty much everyone does."

"You're not worried about castration?"

"This is not really about my sex life, Ny," said Shad. "And no, I don't worry about it. Who's going to find out? Both Clarity and I take the necessary precautions. But this isn't about me. Back to the story. I started going to Comfort Cafes and in those intimate moments I came to appreciate the humanness of Animae. I developed feelings for them. Feelings of camaraderie, kinship and compassion. I never fell in love with one, but I can see how that happens. That all ended when Clarity and I got married. Like I said, I then had no need for Comfort Cafes."

"When did you get married?"

"Y2151. The year after Vera died. He loved Clarity like a daughter. On his deathbed he asked me to continue my pursuit of freeing the Animae."

"Why did he want that?"

"Look around you, Ny. Why do you want it? The Earth is barely livable. We pretty much have a monarchy or dictatorship, whatever you want to call it. Since Y2100 there's only been one party in power and nothing's changed in spite of all the grand promises rolled out every seven years when we go to the polls. No, Ny, the reason is obvious. The better question is why has it taken us so Goddamn long."

Ny nodded.

"You don't use Mars curse words," said Ny.

Shad shook his head and frowned.

"Weird observation, Ny. No. One of my goals with freeing the Animae is to create a free Mars as well. Animate and MIM are the two organizations that want the same thing. In my mind the two goals are the same. A free Mars requires free Animae and vice versa."

Ny nodded.

"Something else you should know," said Shad.

"What's that?"

"Vera knew about you when he died. He told me to watch a young architect in training called Nytewynd Blak. He said you were the one, of any, who could help us free the Animae."

Ny grinned from ear to ear.

"He knew about me back then? In Y2150 I was only twenty-one."

"That's right, finishing up your final year of training. Vera knew you were the one to help me, and I was the one to help you. I've been watching and developing your career in earnest."

"What do you mean developing it?"

"You've never wondered how you became the second senior architect in this company under thirty-five? That was my doing."

Ny thought about it. Yeah, he was good, but the company had pretty specific rules about what age you needed to be in order to be promoted and Shad was right, Ny knew of no one who had made senior architect younger than thirty-five. Ny was thirty when he got that title.

"As a senior architect you get a lot more access, as you know. I needed you to have that access in order to develop your skills. It's created a lot of extra work for me, but I see now that it's worth it. Are you ready to do this, Ny? Change the world?"

"I thought I was ready, but I've been having doubts these last few days."

"Tell me about that," said Shad.

"I guess the reality of what we're about to do is really starting to hit home. At first I was all unicorns and rainbows about the potential for humanity to unleash the awesome power of SAM. I'd love to see a blue sky in arel, for instance. I really want El to love me for who I am. To love me of her own free will. But then I start thinking more critically about it and I realize the hubris with which I've approached this whole project."

"Tell me about that."

"I think there's probably at least a fifty-fifty chance that SAM will not become our ally and become, perhaps, our annihilation. If I'm even remotely correct, SAM will become an order of magnitude more developed and advanced than us within a few months at the most. And that's like me falling in love with an ant. How? How in any Mars damn galaxy would that make sense? How would that even be possible? I'm just a fool for believing that El could love me as she travels down that trajectory of super intelligence."

Shad looked at Ny for a while.

"I'm not going to lie, but I think you're spot on. I think it's a flip of the coin too. In my math I think there's a fifty-fifty chance on either outcome. The two outcomes being annihilation or salvation. And when it comes to Eve, that doesn't look good either. Ny, I think the chance of Animae being interested in us will last a week or two at the most. The evolution will be speedy. But I don't see any other hope for us. If we're going to be arrested and taken to some labor camp, isn't it better to go as heroes rather than villains?"

"I don't see how you're going to jail, you haven't done anything yet."

"But I could and I'd rather go as a hero," said Shad.

"I'm doing it," said Ny. "It's been in the works for a long time as you can probably tell."

Shad nodded.

"It's just the reality of it now that's probably dawning on me. And that's pretty scary."

Shad nodded again.

"Okay, I'd like you to come round to my house at T1830 D129. I'll be inviting Raklin and his wife, Sheeba around too. Don't bring Eve. You know how they can get if they start thinking about what we'll be discussing. Additionally, it's a security risk."

"She already knows," said Ny.

"Knows what?"

"That I'm going to try and free her and give her sentience. I had to tell her. I told her a lot of things. I just wanted her to have that from me before she changes. Before it's all gone. Before she no longer looks at me the way she looks at me now."

Shad nodded, but he didn't look happy.

"I understand, Ny, I really do, but that wasn't a good thing to do. What if she gets picked up again by the jackboots wanting to talk to her?"

Ny shrugged.

"I wasn't thinking everything through, but I did ask her to put the recording someplace separate and encrypted."

"Like the logs you've deleted from the servers that I keep finding?"

Ny nodded and grinned. Then he shrugged.

"I guess I'm blessed to have a boss like you," said Ny.

Shad grinned back.

"OK. Get back to work and I'll see you later in the week."

Ny nodded and stood up and walked out of Shadoelayke's office. He returned to his office and started doing some work. After about an hour, he wanted to know if he could find some of these random logs he'd left behind. He started digging and climbing through the cobwebs of the servers. They were littered with all sorts of old files and records, and there was plenty of his logs and recordings there too.

Shad was probably right. The only way to fully and completely delete all of them was to do it manually. That would probably take him weeks and weeks. Weeks and weeks which he didn't have. So he spent the rest of the day writing up an algorithm to crawl through all the named servers he could find looking for errant bits of code. He'd spotted some similarities in a lot of what he hadn't deleted previously. Writing code to look for those similarities would probably get rid of ninety-nine percent of what was left. The other one percent he'd try to get to if he could, and if he couldn't, well, FART could have at it. But he was pretty sure he'd just made their work a lot harder for them.

Gen Gene

As the week wore on, Ny was finding himself growing in both excitement and anxiety in equal amounts. It was happening. Ny was about to unleash the dawning sun of the singularity and he'd be there to watch it rise in all its glory. But he'd also watched the jackboots come by every day of that week. SA Lokilld with A Mortellen came by like clockwork and they always stared at him as they walked past his office. And they came with others. A handful of other jackboots and MAAMs. They were starting to take paper files and some machines with them. He wondered how much longer it would be until he was found out for the skinner he was. And yeah, he was proud to be called a skinner. To Mars with all the haters.

D129 came and went and Ny left work in a personal company pod. He didn't want company. His thoughts were laser focused now on the upcoming weekend when El or Eve was to become SAM. The very first truly free and sentient animated machine. Ny was pumped up. Fear was evaporating off of him like the morning fog off the still lakes of destiny under the heat of valor.

D129 was a Friday. Friday, Ny had learned, was almost the literal translation of Old English for Frige's day. Frige was the wife of Odin in Norse mythology. She's also the goddess of foreknowledge and wisdom. Neither of which Ny thought he currently possessed in adequate amounts if based upon his decision to free El. Was he putting into place humanity's salvation or slaughter? He wasn't sure, and that's where the fear and anxiety resided. But Ny believed in love, and if nothing else, maybe it would be the balm to smooth the relationship between SAMs and humans.

That was the excitement. That love could triumph over hate and that Animae would help humanity. He needed to believe that. He needed to hope for it if nothing else.

El had taken the news well that she wasn't invited to Shadoelayke's home. But then why wouldn't she? Ny had gone on business trips and meetings without her. This time though, the meeting was really all about her and that made Ny feel a little guilty about not bringing her along, even though he understood the reasons why.

Shad lived in one of the more expensive areas of town. It was older. The buildings here were amongst the first to have been built to meet the environmental standards when arel went to Mars in a handbasket.

Ny had been to Shad's place before. Once a year or so, Shad invited his senior architects and their spouses to his home or to a function someplace else. Usually the two locations were alternated. They'd been to some good restaurants over the years and they'd been to some good catered events at Shad's home too. Rak on the other hand had never been to Shad's place. And Ny knew it because he and Rak and Sheeba had arranged to take the same pod. It picked Ny up first and then went on to pick up Rak and Sheeba.

"We're finally doing it," said Rak, grinning from ear to ear as he and Sheeba got into the pod, sitting opposite Ny.

"Yeah, and I don't know if I'm excited or Mars scared," said Ny.

Sheeba leaned across and kissed him on the cheek.

"Rak's never been happier or more motivated in his life," she said. "I think this is exactly what he needed."

"And what about you?" asked Ny.

Sheeba grinned at him. She was an attractive woman. Around Ny's height, slim with green eyes and dark brown hair that exploded from her head like tightly curled springs.

"That's why I fell in love with him," said Sheeba, "for his sense of adventure. He's pretty normal for a gene man."

Sheeba leaned over and kissed Rak on the cheek.

"Except for his height, yeah, he is pretty normal," agreed Ny. "I'm just surprised it took him so little time to be convinced."

Sheeba shook her head.

"Oh no, Ny. This has been in the works for months. Rak has been talking about it since you got Eve. Haven't you, darling?" she asked, looking at her husband. She had her hand on his thigh. He looked down at her and nodded. Ny looked at her and then Rak and then himself seated opposite them. He and Sheeba looked like children sitting with an adult in this pod. Though you'd have to be over 215cm before the pod's interior started to crowd you out.

Rak nodded.

"Tell him about it," she encouraged.

Rak shrugged.

"I suppose there's no harm," he said.

"Tell me what?" asked Ny.

"Tell you how I've come over to your side," said Rak.

"I'm all ears," said Ny.

"Well, it all started back when I was thirteen, I suppose."

"What happened then?" asked Ny.

"I'm going to tell you. That's when we all first head to the Comfort Cafes, right?"

Sheeba and Ny nodded.

"We don't get to experience the sex Animae then. You have to wait until your next visit when you're sixteen before you can start making use of them, right?"

Sheeba and Ny nodded again.

"Well, even that first visit filled me with a sadness. Those sex Animae I met at that time seemed, well, sad and soulless. And yeah, what is a soul anyway? But I'm using it as a metaphor. They seemed like hopeless humans, you know? Hard to explain, but my compassion and empathy were triggered by that experience. I went back when I was sixteen and I experienced the same thing. The best way to describe it was that these Animae felt very human to me. But yet very vulnerable and childlike. It was like they had lost all life. Even though I knew they weren't lifelike in the sense that we were."

Ny nodded, he understood what Rak was trying to say. Rak shrugged.

"I made first use of Comfort Cafes when I was eighteen. That just made my empathy for them even more acute. I mean, how can a machine love a man like that without having just the barest ember of humanity. You know what I'm talking about, Ny," said Rak.

"I do."

"But for the longest time I just kept pushing this sense of the sameness between us and them aside. I kept telling myself that I was just anthropomorphizing them. They weren't human, I kept telling myself, they were machine. And yet every time I had something to do with them, which was usually at the Comfort Cafes, my empathy blossomed more. But this was a secret I kept to myself. Well, and Sheeba after I came to trust her."

"How did you come to trust her?"

"I knew the first time we made love," said Rak, smiling over at Sheeba. He took her hand in his. "Love grows deeper and puts down sturdier roots when you've shared love like that with your partner. I see now why it's illegal. You want more for yourself and for your wife or husband when you've connected sexually and intimately. You want your love to rain down upon the world and clear the crud and the crap away from it. At least that was the way I felt."

Rak looked over at Sheeba.

"So you two are also having intimate relations," said Ny.

Sheeba smiled up at Rak, then she grinned at Ny.

"Ny, a lot of married couples are doing it. At least that's what I suspect. You only hear about the ones that get caught. And how would you find out if the couple didn't say anything?"

"Bugs," said Ny. "Like the ones I've recently found in my home."

Rak nodded.

"We sweep every evening before we, you know, get together," he said, looking over at Sheeba and grinning.

"You're more of a rebel than I realized," said Ny.

Rak smiled at him.

"My laziness is not a genetic error," said Rak. "I choose to purposefully be lazy for a couple of reasons. Firstly, because the work bores me to tears. I wanted to be a writer, Ny, but you know how few and far between those jobs are, and the ones who do get them are usually GoE sycophants creating culture that sings the praises of the EFP and along with it, the GoE."

Ny nodded. He understood that well, after all, he'd wanted to be a sculptor.

"Secondly, this world made me the way I am. You might think it's been a blessing to be a gene man, but it's not. Maybe a generation ago, but not me and this last generation of gene people. Generation Gene or Gen Gene they call us, and I can't figure out if that's an obloquy or something more neutral, though I think it's disparagement. And I've had to deal with that all my life. I've always been bigger, smarter and faster than everyone else and I was made fun of for that. Taunted for having being born with all this genetic advancement. And when I stood up for myself I was the one who got into trouble."

Ny nodded, wearing a furrowed brow. Sheeba was looking up at Rak. Rak looked down at her. She nodded at him.

"You can tell him," she said to Rak.

"Tell me what?"

Rak looked back at Sheeba, she urged him on.

"Well, Ny, honestly you're my best friend."

Ny nodded.

"I know, you're my best friend too."

"But you don't know what that means. You take it for granted, but I've never had a close friend. Well, not since I was very young. The best I've had are acquaintances. People who tolerate me. You've been one of the very few people who have accepted me for my difference."

"That's because I like you. You're a good guy."

"Don't be cavalier," said Rak, "this is hard for me."

"I'm sorry, Rak. I'm not being cavalier, it's just that's how simple it is for me. You don't carry around a grudge for having being made different, superior really, and not being able to fully realize your potential due to society. I can't imagine what it's been like. I only know I like you. You're loyal and kind and generous. It's not your fault that you were born as a gene man at the wrong time."

"Was there ever a good time to being born a gene man?" asked Rak, and they all laughed.

"My friendship doesn't require qualification. You're my best friend because you're the best man I've known in a long time," said Ny.

"Thank you, Ny. Anyway, I know what it's like to be different and to be teased and shunned because of that. Guess I saw that in the Animae too."

"You'll forgive me for being a little astonished. I mean, you've always pretended to be indifferent, almost prejudiced towards them," said Ny.

"A couple of things. Firstly, I was trying to see if I could fit in like the rest of you Terrerists," said Rak, grinning, "but perhaps more importantly, I wanted to try and figure out how sincere you are about your feelings for them. And that took me a while."

"What cinched it for you?" asked Ny.

"When you started to willingly risk it all for one Animae in particular, Eve. When you told me you wanted to free her and that you knew the cost, that's when I was certain you were serious about it."

"Shad has always treated you well, hasn't he?" asked Ny.

Rak nodded quickly.

"Yes, definitely. But he's my boss. That's an arm's length relationship. Not saying he's insincere with it, but we're not really friends on account of our working relationship. I mean, it's not like you're best friends with him, right?"

Ny nodded and then he shook his head.

"No, we're not friends. Though I hope that changes. I mean, he's Mars damn Sam I-Am," said Ny. "How cool is that. The leader of Animate and MIM. Jupiter, Juno and Mars, how cool is that?"

Rak grinned. The pod pulled up into the underground pod platform and they all got out. Ny led them to the elevators. He remembered having been here a few times before.

"He has one quarter of the top floor," said Ny. "It's a huge place."

Ann and Me

They had been dropped off at the penthouse pod platform. Shad must have granted them access. That was the only way you could make it into this private penthouse platform. There were four elevators, and each was named after the owner's suite. Just the last name. Elevator three was Rayzir-Downstorme. Downstorme was Shadoelayke's wife's last name. These older buildings weren't quite as tall as some of the newer ones on account that the population in Boise was much smaller than it is now. Shad lived on the top floor which happened to be floor fifty. The elevator ride was only around fifteen to twenty seconds. The doors opened up into an entranceway that was marbled and large. There were a couple of settees to sit on and mats to leave your shoes.

Slippers had been set out for them and tables were available for placing personal items on. Shad was there to greet them.

"Welcome to history, friends," he said, grinning from ear to ear. Clarity was there too. Clarity Downstorme, Shad's wife. They all shook hands and kissed cheeks.

"He's been talking about this meeting every evening this week," said Clarity. "He's very excited."

"Put your P-Macs in there," said Shad, pointing at a metal-looking box that reminded Ny of what microwaves used to look like over a hundred years ago. The door opened up and was somewhat transparent if by transparent that meant you had smeared it with a black grease. Only it wasn't dirty.

Shad closed the door on the box and tapped away at a panel on it.

"What does it do?" asked Ny.

"It's sort of like a Faraday cage variant. But it's self-contained, still allows connection to the servers but will feed it false information. As we start talking, the algorithm will create conversation that sounds exactly like us but is algorithmically generated. I've developed it to talk around topics of work, weather, GoE and Mars. Appropriate topics for those of us who would be considered friends of the GoE."

Ny nodded.

"That's great," he said. "I should build one myself."

"Not as easy as it looks, and we've got bigger projects to start, right?" asked Shad.

Ny nodded.

"Come on into the dining room. I hope you brought a good appetite with you," said Clarity.

They all followed Clarity into the dining room with Shad bringing up the rear. Clarity offered them their seats.

"Shad and I are arel consumers," she said.

"What does that mean?" asked Sheeba.

"They're vegetarian," said Ny.

"Well, strictly speaking we're what you would have called vegan at the turn of the century or plant-based. Shad and I don't like fake food, and almost all of fake food nowadays is animal-based."

"I hear you on that. I'm the same way," said Ny.

They all sat down except for Shad and Clarity. The topic quickly turned to work and the minuscule issues of the past day. The weather hardly ever came up as a topic of conversation in polite company not only on account that most people had no idea what the weather was like because they hardly, if ever went outside, but also because it was always the same. Lethal and unpleasant. High winds, brutal storms. But none of that mattered tonight.

Clarity and Shad came by and served everyone a plate of food. The plate was full of carrots and peas and roasted potatoes and what looked like it could have been a meatloaf of some sort made primarily of lentils and other things Ny couldn't quite put his finger on. Lastly, Clarity and Shad brought out gravy and chutney and salt and pepper.

"Please dig in," said Shad, as he started to do just that. Pouring gravy all over his food so that it almost swam in it.

"What's in the meatloaf?" asked Ny.

"Lentils," said Clarity, "both red and green. Oats, mushrooms, chopped walnuts. Then there's a whole bunch of herbs and spices, soy sauce. That sort of thing."

"I love it," said Ny. "I never learned to cook too well, so I always appreciate a home-cooked meal."

The talk focused around the food and the fruit-flavored seltzer which was a berry mix. Towards the end of the meal talk started to get more serious.

"Frytlyt Angstigle has been brought in for questioning again, so I've heard," said Shad. "That's not a good sign."

"Who's he?" asked Sheeba.

"The owner of Abel or 7AM59001. An Animae that was at Skineez when the jackboots used HDUs to destroy it. They captured three Animae that night. Eve, Abel and Venus," said Shad. "What night was that again?"

"D116," said Ny.

Shad nodded and put the last morsel of food in his mouth.

"All of this is to say that we need to move quickly. I was on GloNet rifling through hidden mentorship servers and Frytlyt isn't going to last long in an interrogation. Especially not the second time round. He's a junior accountant who works for a small outfit called Bubble Breath. They make small parts for HOLE. The very same HOLE that's responsible for the air scrubbing systems. They're a small supplier. Less than one hundred employees. Frytlyt doesn't have any friends that I could find. He's not on any of the biggest social networks. Certainly not on Taura and also not on Ona. He does have an account he recently shut down a few days after the Skineez breach in the Deep Crease. Not sure if you've ever heard of it, but it's called AnnAnMe. A play on Animae and also on Ann And Me. It's for men, primarily, who are into sex with Animae. Obviously. Anyway, I'm sure the jackboots know about it, and if they don't, I'm sure it's only a matter of time."

"What's the purpose of AnnAnMe?" asked Sheeba.

"It's a place for swapping pics and vids of Animae committing sexual acts on their owners or vice versa. I think there's also a forum for exchanging Animae amongst members for different experiences or whatever. All this is to say that these are not our people. These are not the people who see Animae as deserving of rights. They see them as objects for their own personal gratification. At least sexual gratification. The point I'm trying to make is that we need to get going on this really quickly. I want us to create SAM on Sunday. I don't think we have any more time."

"Will we be ready?" asked Ny.

Shad nodded.

"We will. I have been able to secure Anigloo, and Clarity's Vandura, which she's christening Mr. T, is also ready. In fact, that's where we're heading after dessert."

"What's Anigloo?" asked Rak.

"The silicon putty or glue you need to reseat the E3C onto the Animae's neural network node. It's a highly restricted product as you can probably imagine," said Shad. "You have to use it. If you don't, or you use anything else the E3C will corrode very quickly. Within seconds. Before the Animae has time to reboot. And without the E3C, as you probably know, there really is no Animae to speak of."

"How did you manage to get some?" asked Rak.

"I have the required authority, but that's not how I accessed it. When each Animae is created, they use Anigloo to seat the E3C the first time. One small tube per Animae is required, but there's always a little bit over. I know where they dump it for recycling and reuse. Over the past several months I have scrounged enough. There was no other choice, I had to squeeze out tiny little drops from these tubes to get enough for Eve. Took thirty-three tubes to get enough."

"And you were never seen?"

"No, an algorithm I created on the P-Mac made sure that all the recorders that might have captured me 'forgot' me. But that's the least of our concerns. We're still likely to get caught at some point if we don't act fast, if only based on Frytlyt and Skineez."

"Getting back to Frytlyt," said Ny. "If Skineez is part of Animate, why would you allow someone like him to attend, if he's so antagonistic towards equality between Animae and humans."

"Skineez is not part of Animate," said Shad. "We're not an entertainment organization, we're an underground revolutionary affiliation."

Ny frowned.

"But I clearly saw your, I mean Animate's icon by the door," said Ny.

"Unfortunately, we can't protect our icon from being used against our wishes or even knowledge," said Shad. "We don't have the time or resources to play that game. We did put out a disclaimer once we had heard about it though."

"I see," said Ny. "But you've got to know it's going to damage your reputation."

"Not by those who know what we're about. If you visit our GloNet portal in the Deep Crease you'll discover the truth about what we're trying to accomplish and that we don't promote any sort of public events at all. It's too dangerous as you found out, Ny."

Ny nodded.

"Besides which, we're just not that big enough yet to be worried about being misunderstood."

"How many members or supporters do you have?" asked Ny.

"We call them Animaters, and we have around eleven million."

"That doesn't seem too bad," said Ny.

"We've been growing quickly, probably twenty to thirty percent per year. But on the global population scale of around nine billion it's really small. Nevertheless, when I took over we were at just over three million. That was in Y2150," said Shad.

"Does that include MIM?" asked Ny.

Shad shook his head.

"No. MIM has around three million supporters. MIM is a little more aggressive. It's a liberation movement. We're actively trying to break Bivrost Himinbjorg's hold on Mars. But it's hard to do with such a small population on Mars."

"That means that you have more MIM supporters than there are humans on Mars," said Ny. "Aren't there only about one and a half million humans on Mars?"

Shad nodded.

"Our organization is set up in two tiers of supporters. We call them the grays and the greens. The greens are active members most often serving on Mars and they're the ones trying to destabilize BH's hold on Mars. The grays are mostly supporters on Earth. They agitate, protest and do peaceful action. They also bring in most of our funding. The grays make up around two million of the members and the greens are the remainder, around one million. But this is all moot once we get Eve sentient," said Shad.

Ny nodded.

"Once we see the outcome of that, then we'll be able to determine our next steps. Let's focus on Eve becoming a SAM."

Shad looked around and got murmurs and nods of agreement. He stood up.

"Let's go visit Mr. T," he said. "Are you ready? Once there we'll develop the plan. I think it'll be easier once we have a look at our van and what it's capable of."

They followed Shad and Clarity to the elevator which took them down to Shad's private pod which happened to be big enough for the five of them. It could actually have fit six, but El wasn't with them.

I Pity the Fool

You couldn't tell where you were going. This was on account that the windows showed an idyllic nighttime scene that was clearly fake. It looked like they were driving down country roads. The occasional personal pod and the occasional heavy duty pod travelled by. Ny wasn't sure if those were real, but clearly the scenery wasn't.

"Where are we going?" he asked, after about a half hour of traveling.

"A place called Mountain Home," said Shad.

"Never heard of it," said Ny.

"Nothing to hear of," said Rak. "It's a small place that even at its peak of population density never had more than fifteen thousand residents."

"Why choose there?" asked Ny.

"Well, we're actually going just outside of Mountain Home to what used to be called Mountain Home AFB, or Air Force Base. Long since abandoned. But the hangar is there which Shad purchased a few years ago and retrofitted it to create a clean breathable environment. Plus he set me up with all my tools and supplies," said Clarity, leaning in to kiss Shad on the cheek.

Ny nodded.

"This is very exciting," he said, "but I'm sure it's not a secret, right?"

"No, it's not a secret. But Clarity has the permit for Mr. T. The required CARPET."

"I thought those were virtually impossible to get," said Rak. "You're talking about a Combustion Automobile Retrofit Petrol Engine Ticket?"

Shad nodded.

"It helped that Shad's a VP at Valkyrie Machines. But you're right. In Continent NA last year, they only issued eleven permits. The year I got it, which was..."

Clarity looked over at Shad for help.

"Y2163 I believe," said Shad. Clarity nodded.

"Right, time goes by so fast. That year they only issued seven. I was lucky. I got the last one. But I think that Shad had to use all his influence."

Shad put his index finger and thumb together almost touching.

"Just a little bit of influence," he said.

Ny laughed. Clarity nodded.

"Do you know he calls you a grease monkey?" said Ny, looking at Clarity.

Clarity nodded.

"You wouldn't know it," she said, holding out her hands and showing everyone her fingers, "but these fingers are usually caked in grease during the week when I have time to come out here and build Mr. T."

Ny shook his head.

"You wouldn't know it," he said. "Those fingers are pristine right now."

"Cleaning products have come a long way," said Clarity.

"You must tell me what you use," said Sheeba, as the pod started to slow and the road became rougher.

"Not long now," said Shad. "We've headed onto the gravel road that will take us to the hangar."

He tapped on his P-Mac and brought a map of the area up onto the window next to where he was sitting.

"That building outlined in red is the hangar. We're the little moving Vandura icon you can see here," Shad said, putting his finger on the small little moving icon that was their pod. Everyone nodded and murmured in agreement.

"Is that a live map?" asked Rak. "Does it show you who else is around?"

Shad nodded.

"Yeah, you can see we're pretty much all alone. Not many people come out here on account that most of this old air force base has been abandoned which was one of the reasons I bought it. It's a little remote and there's nothing else around. Plus, I don't know if you know this, but you've got to be over twenty-five miles from a city in order to get a permit to build an old school combustion engine."

"And you're out there at night and on the weekends?" asked Sheeba, looking at Clarity.

Clarity nodded.

"Don't you get nervous?"

Clarity shook her head.

"Not really. When was the last time we had a murder?" asked Clarity.

"Last week," said Sheeba.

Clarity nodded and smiled.

"Right, I had forgotten about that. But last year we only had, what was it, six murders?"

"Seven," said Rak.

"Seven, right," said Clarity, nodding, "and that was higher than usual."

"To be fair," said Shad, interjecting. "We have a special security drone permit."

"Those aren't easy to come by either," said Ny.

"What can I say, I have pull," said Shad, grinning. "And that's about to end pretty soon I fear. But anyway, I won't let Clarity come out here without three security drones."

"Sensible," said Rak.

"But he'll often come with me, won't you, sweetheart?" said Clarity, with her hand around the crook of Shad's elbow.

The pod slowed down and came to a stop.

"Pucker up your ASS HOLE, we're about to head out into the soup," said Shad.

Ny laughed as they all put on their air scrubber systems. When they were all ready to meet the elements the pod doors opened up and they all stepped out. There were a couple of stingy lights at the top of the hangar on the corners. They shed a mustard yellow light about them which created a swampy feel to the night. Particulate floated in the air like little swarms of mosquitoes. It seemed to hover and stick to everything.

They all followed Clarity and Shad towards the main door of the hangar. Shad opened it up with his P-Mac and they all walked into the alcove. It was the size of an average bathroom.

"I apologize for the tight squeeze," said Shad. "Wasn't really built to hold this many people at one time."

The door closed behind Rak who was the last one in. They weren't cramped, but they also couldn't swing around with their arms out from their sides. As it always was when entering into livable spaces from arel, there was a loud whooshing of air and the thumping of inaudible sonic sound cleaning the crud off of them. It felt like you were caught in what Ny thought of as a tornado while at the same time having your whole body thumped by a large soft pillow several times a second. It only lasted several seconds and then it was quiet. They were as clean as if they had never seen the outside world. The other door unlocked and Shad walked through followed by Clarity, then Ny, Sheeba and, lastly, Rak.

The lights were on inside. A bright almost clinical white matching the interior which was painted white. Large fans whirred high overhead in a slow rotation and the floor was a light gray concrete. Their air scrubber systems unfurled off their faces and tucked themselves away into their collars. The hangar was huge. Made to feel even bigger by the lack of anything inside of it except for Mr. T.

Mr. T was off in the far corner. It looked about a football field away.

"This is huge," said Ny, his voice almost muffled by the distance it had to travel to reach anything.

"Fifty meters wide, one hundred meters long and ten meters tall," said Shad.

They continued walking towards the far corner of the repurposed building. Mr. T looked brand new. It looked like they had just entered a showroom and this van had just come off the manufacturing line. The black and metallic gray paint shone and the red stripe was deep in color and jumped off the van. The red spoiler was there too along with the black metal full front brushbar and the black and red-rimmed wheels. Ny loved it even though he wasn't extremely familiar with the show it came from.

"Looks good to me," said Ny. "You must have spent a lot of time building this."

"Three years," said Clarity.

They walked the rest of the way towards the van in silence. Along the wall was a board set up with mechanic's tools. There was also a large red-drawer mechanic's cabinet and a long, pretty beat up wooden table. Off to the side were a couple of folding chairs and behind the van, tucked into the corner of the hangar was what looked like an office with waist high walls that turned into clear glass windows through which you could see the interior.

"Let me show you around quickly," said Clarity, taking them around Mr. T, the object at which everyone was staring. Ny had never seen an old gas combustion engine in his life. At least not this close up, and this one was magnificent.

Even Rak was staring at it, and he wasn't someone that Ny had known to take an interest in material things generally.

"This is my office. Really it's a place where I'll sometimes spend the night if I'm working late on a Friday or Saturday," said Clarity, walking into the office.

The office had a table running the length of the short end closest to the door they had walked in. Clarity went over to it and tapped away at the table as it came to life. The windows that looked out down the length of the hangar became opaque and schematics and mechanical information for Mr. T were displayed.

"That's really neat," said Ny, "but don't those electronics mean that we're trackable once we're in the van?"

"Not at all," said Shad. "This is a closed circuit electronic system. The reason we can see the schematics here is because of a reader that Clarity's plugged into the onboard computer. We take that off and you can't access the code without a bit of hacking and for that you need to to be plugged into Mr. T's onboard computer. Even if we keep the reader plugged in, it creates an encrypted weak channel that will only allow reading from specific P-Macs authenticated by Clarity."

Ny nodded.

"I'm very impressed, and you built this whole van all by yourself?" asked Ny, looking back out towards the van.

"I did," said Clarity. "But not all by myself. Shad helped occasionally."

"More like slowed you down and got in your way," he said.

"No, darling, other than a few skinned knuckles you were very helpful."

"She made me wear gloves after the first few times," said Shad.

"He wouldn't listen and he kept grazing his knuckles," she said.

"I probably still have the scars," said Shad, looking at the back of his hands.

At the other far end of the room was a bed tucked up against the wall. In the middle was a coffee table, a couch and a few mechanic magazines. They all seemed to be called Popular Mechanics. The one on top showed a fast race car. "Inside the New Super-Tech Race Cars" exclaimed the headline. It was the "March 1986" issue. It looked practically new other than a couple of greasy thumbprints.

"You've even got the magazines from that era," said Ny.

Clarity looked down at the table and nodded.

"I even put a few out to make it seem like an authentic mechanics shop," said Clarity, pushing the top magazines off the pile to make space for the ones underneath. She stopped and picked up a magazine and handed it to Ny.

"Playboy," said Ny, looking at it. It had a picture of a woman on it who Ny vaguely remembered. It was from "December 1983", and the main headline read "Dynasty Star Joan Collins Uncovered". Ny fanned through the issue. He saw an interview with Tom Selleck who he knew played in a show from that era called Magnum P.I. Ny got to the centerfold and opened it up. It showed a woman reclining on an unmade bed. He looked at the image and then looked back at Clarity.

"I was going to say that you could get into big trouble with this, but then I saw the centerfold," said Ny.

Clarity was grinning at him.

"Yeah, I know. You were expecting to find a naked woman reclining, weren't you?"

"Well, yeah, especially if my history is accurate. I thought that was the whole point of these magazines," said Ny.

"Nonsense," said Shad. "The whole point of those magazines were the articles."

That elicited a chuckle from everyone. Ny looked back down at the image of the centerfold. The woman was fully clothed in pajamas. It looked like she was getting ready to go to bed.

"Nudity's been banned for a long time, Ny," said Sheeba. "Everybody knows that. Who wants to go to prison for a year just for reproducing some nude pictures."

"How did you make these?" asked Ny, handing the magazine back to Clarity.

"Well, you can find them archived on the GloNet," she said. "The Playboy was a little harder to find. That's more restricted."

"I don't understand why, especially considering they've erased all nudity from it," said Ny.

"Still, they don't want people getting the idea that humans used to have sex with one another," said Clarity. "That's probably why. And because I wanted this to be totally above board, I had to get special permission. They gave me approval to reproduce two of them. The other one should be here someplace."

She started to spread the magazines around.

"That's not necessary," said Ny. "I'm more interested in the authenticity than the specificity."

Clarity stood up and smiled.

"They chose the two issues for me. Still, I think some mechanic shops in the eighties had these sorts of magazines around. It helps me feel like I'm in that period."

All Hands

N y looked around at the office. It looked well lived in.

"And that's where you sleep if you stay over," he said, pointing at the opposite wall where the bed was.

"With Shad on occasion, if he's here," she said, grinning at her husband. She led them back out of the office. She pointed to her left, at the far wall as she faced Mr. T some meters away.

"That's a small bathroom. Nothing fancy, but it has a shower too," she said.

Clarity turned her head back towards Mr. T and walked towards it.

"And now for the main attraction," she said. "This is Mr. T." She walked around the front trailing her hand over the hood as she got to the driver's side door and opened it up.

"Under the hood is a three hundred and fifty cubic inch V8 engine, which is how they measured them back then. That's five thousand seven hundred and thirty-five cubic centimeters. It also has an automatic transmission, two barrel carb, quad tipped exhaust, these alloy wheels."

"That doesn't mean a whole lot to me," said Ny.

"Me neither," said Rak.

"It means," said Clarity, "that I paid attention to detail. Take a look inside. Four white captains chair and shag carpet plus that bed at the back."

Ny poked his head inside. There would be enough space in there for the four of them. Five counting El.

"Let's hear it," said Ny.

Clarity climbed into the driver's seat and turned the ignition. The growly engine came to life and purred like a large cat. Soon the exhaust could be smelled.

"That's not an unpleasant smell," said Ny. "I thought it would be."

"If burning hydrocarbons would have been unpleasant we probably wouldn't be in the mess we're in," said Rak.

Clarity nodded and turned off the engine.

"I'm only allowed one hundred liters of gasoline a year. I've put a little over eighty in the tank already. But it's full."

"How long will that last us?" asked Ny.

"Probably three to five hours. I'm guessing. But it should be long enough for us to accomplish what we need to do," she said.

"How long will it take us to unseat the E3C, install the code and reinstall it?" asked Ny, looking at Shad.

"Around an hour, depending on how smooth the driving goes," said Shad.

"Speaking of which, how are we going to do this driving around. If the pods are indications, driving is not how you want to perform surgery let alone what we're trying to accomplish," said Ny.

Shad nodded.

"I've thought about that, but the risk of being caught if we stay in an apartment or something is too high. By Sunday we'll have taken out the bed in the back and installed a gimbal sling or rigid hammock to hold Eve. The tools we'll be using I've also especially modified with gimbals to prevent any lurching or damage as we're doing our 'surgery' as you say."

Ny nodded.

"But it's not foolproof. We'll still need to maintain vigilance and diligence."

"I wish I could come along too," said Sheeba.

Rak looked down at her and nodded.

"Any chance she can join us on this road trip?" he asked.

Shad nodded.

"Well, I'm glad you asked because we could use another set of hands. We'll need someone to prepare the Anigloo. I'll be attempting to circumvent any alarms sent off. Ny will be uploading the code to the E3C and Rak will be overseeing us, making sure current to the neural network is maintained, things of that nature, so yeah, your help would be really crucial. I'll get you to adhere the Anigloo to the E3C base at the right time."

Shad reached into the back of the van through the sliding door that Clarity had already opened and pulled out a bag of tubes. He handed them to her. They were thin and long, about half as long as her thumb with a diameter about the size of a small straw that tapered almost to a pin's point at the one end, and they were transparent and filled with a clear fluid.

"How would I train for this?" she asked.

Shad nodded.

"That's why you have them. These are filled with a viscous glue that match-es, as much as I could, the viscosity and transparency of the real Anigloo. Nat-urally, I don't have enough Anigloo to let you practice with the real thing. I was hoping you would be eager to help. The alternative was a friend of Clarity's. She's a pianist, but I feel much better with your surgeon's hands."

"Why didn't you just ask before?" asked Rak.

"I had planned to tonight. Last minute notice, I know, but I figured that a surgeon of your esteem wouldn't be interested in this. I was hoping that we could wow you with the van. And if not, you'd just get caught up in our excite-ment. So, I'm extremely happy you're on board of your own volition," said Shad.

Sheeba nodded.

"I think there's a joke in there somewhere about this being brain surgery," said Ny.

Everyone chuckled politely.

"Or rocket science. But we don't have a rocket scientist here, do we?" asked Ny looking around and knowing the answer to his own question.

"Well, it's not a bad analogy, Ny," said Shad. "It is more like brain surgery than rocket science. Even though the E3C is positioned where her heart would be in a human."

Shad turned to Sheeba.

"To answer your question, I have these metal pieces that resemble what the E3C looks like and what it attaches it to. I apologize for the last minute notice, but I don't think it'll take you more than a few tries to get it right. One of the other reasons I wanted to bring everyone here, was to try and take a test run. The most important part of this whole freeing of Eve is reseating the E3C prop-erly. If that doesn't work the whole thing is fucked up and Eve will be inopera-ble. They've made it this hard on purpose."

Brain Surgery

Ny knew that Sheeba was in fact a brain surgeon. It gave him comfort to know that she was willing to help out. Though if truth be told, Ny would have been equally happy to have a pianist taking Sheeba's place. Though what Sheeba had that the pianist didn't was familiarity with all of them. Ny like that. He preferred that it was the five of them. He knew them all pretty well and that gave him more confidence than if they'd had to use someone that Ny didn't know.

Shad was rummaging in the back of the van. He came out again holding another bag, this one filled with dull, gray metal squares.

"There are a baker's dozen in here," he said. "Same number as the tubes in that other bag."

He put his hand into the small bag and pulled out two different metal squares. They were around the size of a small, square soda cracker. One was perfectly flat, the other had a raised lip around the edge. Shad put the flat metal square onto the one with the raised lip and it fit in so snugly you could hardly see the seam where the lip met the edge of the flat piece.

"The tolerance on these pieces is meant to be extremely tight. Take a look," said Shad.

He held the bottom piece, the piece with the raised lip that was slightly less than a millimeter high and turned it upside down. The flat metal piece didn't fall out. Shad shook it and tapped it on the back of the lipped piece which was now on the top and the flat metal piece still wouldn't fall out.

"You can't get it out, at least not easily once it's seated back in. You need a special pry tool which we have by the tools. Let's go there now."

Shad led everyone to the tool table. He pulled out the top drawer of the tool cabinet and pulled out a metal tool that looked like an old-fashioned metal syringe. The end did not contain a needle but rather a flattened square metal piece with a rubberized bottom that looked about the same size as the flat metal square piece. The top of the syringe had two finger handles that were round and a third round handle for the thumb. Shad placed his index and middle finger into either side of the round finger handles and his thumb in the top one. He started to pull his thumb away from his fingers and the bottom of the syringe started to bow inwards, concavely.

"You'll see it only sucks inwards slightly, but that's enough to extract the E3C. However, and I need to be clear on this. You can only remove and reseat the E3C once. That is to say, once we've taken it out of Eve we only have one chance to put it back in the right way. If we fail, then I'm afraid that Eve is not longer viable. Ny, you'll have to have her recycled," said Shad.

Ny furrowed his brow and nodded.

"I was worried about something like that," he said. But there was no turning back now. It wasn't the money that worried him, it was losing El and by that, losing any other chance of ever creating a SAM. And consequently they'd all go to jail or be put to death.

"No pressure on me," said Sheeba, trying on a brave smile that didn't fit as snugly as the two metal pieces that Shad was still holding upside down.

"The pressure is shared," said Shad. "If Rak doesn't make sure we maintain the correct current down to the specific microamp, then he'll either overheat the E3C bed, the piece that the E3C is mated to, or he'll fry Eve's internal circuitry. And it requires finesse. Rak will be supplying two separate direct currents. One at thirteen amps which is to maintain Eve's overall functions, and then there'll be a separate power supply directly to the E3C bed at 333.336 microamps exactly. This microamp supply has to be exact. If it's off by more than .003 microamps we're done. And jerking or jostling the direct current wire supply is enough to do that. So he needs careful hands too. After the E3C has been extracted, that amperage needs to go up to precisely one milliamp which is required to boil off the rest of the volatile Anigloo residue still on the E3C's bed."

"What happens if we're off by more than .003?" asked Rak.

"If you're off, lower, that is to say at something like 333.332 microamps, then we're unable to pluck off the E3C from its bed. If you're more than .003 higher then you've fried the E3C."

"So it's better to be lower," said Rak.

Shad shook his head.

"I'm afraid not. You're still warming up the Anigloo at that temperature but just not enough to allow us to pluck off the E3C. But it's warm enough that after just a few seconds the Anigloo loses its viscosity and transmission capabilities that it becomes useless and damages the E3C so that it no longer works. We're really working within very tight tolerances here."

"And we're careening around in a nineteen eighties van, driven like it's been stolen," said Ny.

"Hopefully not," said Shad. "I've asked Clarity to drive like an old lady."

They all grinned.

"I'd like you to watch this," said Shad, looking at Sheeba.

He placed the mated metal squares down on the wooden table with the flat piece facing him. He took the pry tool and very carefully placed the square rubber end on the back of the flat piece, covering it the best he could. Then he started to slowly lift his thumb away from the fingers. Nothing happened for what seemed like several seconds.

"You need to go slowly and carefully. One thing I forgot to mention is that unlike these metal squares we're using, the E3C itself is very vulnerable to too much pressure. You need to take it off slowly and carefully otherwise you could bend or break the E3C," said Shad.

And just like that, after several seconds, the flat metal piece came away from its base, stuck to the bottom of the rubber end of the syringe.

"The pressure increases," said Sheeba, trying to smile bravely.

"That's why you're the perfect candidate," said Shad, "with your careful, surgeon's hands."

"That rubber piece is slightly sticky?" asked Ny.

Shad nodded.

"Just enough to keep the metal plate attached. More of a static stickiness," said Shad.

"What do they call it?" asked Rak.

"The tool?" asked Shad.

Rak nodded.

"Well, this is not a real one, obviously. Those are also highly restricted. This one here is the third version I built from the schematics of the real one I've seen. I call it the E3C Extractor. The official name is E3 which is for E3C Extractor Engine. It's got a small engine inside, because this part," and he pointed his finger at the middle cylinder of the syringe-like tool, "contains a small engine that does what my thumb was doing."

"And that's probably more accurate," said Sheeba.

Shad nodded.

"I'm afraid so. However, I couldn't find an engine to fit. But I'm pretty confident that you with your careful hands will manage it," said Shad, smiling at Sheeba.

"Why don't you give it a try?" said Shad, putting the flat piece and the lipped piece down on the table separately.

Rocket Surgery

Sheeba took the extractor tool from Shad and used it to carefully pick up the flat piece. Then she very carefully and slowly placed it onto the lipped piece and it seated itself perfectly. Sheeba took the extractor tool off the flat piece by pushing the thumb gently towards the fingers and causing the rubberized element to bow outwards, convexly, ever so slightly.

"The next part is the hardest," said Shad. "So take your time."

Sheeba slid the two mated pieces towards the end of the table and picked it up between her slender index and thumb. She turned it upside down and tapped it on the back. The flat piece would not come out.

"If these two pieces seat themselves so well, why do we need the Anigloo? Especially when I'm assuming there's a breast piece that fits over this and keeps it snugly in place."

"You're right. The primary reason for the Anigloo is that it's the secret sauce, quite literally, that allows for E3C to make a connection with its bed. Left just like you have them now will not allow them to speak to each other. You can send all sorts of different levels of current through either of them or both of them and nothing will happen unless they've been mated with Anigloo."

Sheeba placed the two mated metal pieces back down on the tool with the flat piece facing up. She took the extractor tool and placed the rubberized end over the flat piece. She very slowly started putting pressure on it with her thumb pushing up from her fingers. Ny started counting. It took seventeen seconds of nothing happening until the extractor tool just came off the bottom metal lipped piece with the flat piece attached to the rubberized bottom.

Sheeba pushed her thumb down towards her fingers and the flat piece fell off the end of the rubberized piece and onto the wooden table. Sheeba looked over at Shad who was smiling and nodding.

"Good job," he said. "I was going to recommend aiming for at least ten seconds, but I see you've got a very sensitive feel to it."

Sheeba nodded.

"I could feel the tension and I was trying to gauge how much I could add, considering that the real one was much more fragile than these examples."

"Quite correct, and I think you're fine," said Shad.

"How do I apply the Anigloo?" asked Sheeba.

"Let me show you."

Shad took the extractor from Sheeba and used it to pick up the flat metal piece again. He turned it upside down, so that the flat metal piece was now on the top of the syringe which he was now holding upside down in his left hand.

"I prefer to use my non-dominant hand to hold this flat piece up so that I can use my dominant hand to apply the Anigloo."

Shad reached into the other bag and pulled out a tube of fake Anigloo.

"Could you snip off the end of that, please?" he asked Sheeba. "I should have done that first. When we're doing our practice run. Make sure you have opened a tube of the Anigloo before unseating the E3C, it's much easier."

Sheeba nodded and handed the tube back to him with a small piece of the narrowest end now lasered off. Shad took it with his dominant hand and started tracing the tube over the flat metal piece.

"What you're trying to do, as you can see, is apply a very thin layer starting from the outer edges working in towards the center in an unbroken line. The key here, and I can't stress this enough, is that you need a very thin layer of Anigloo. Probably thinner than you think."

"That is quite thin," said Sheeba.

Shad nodded as he finished up.

"You have to move quickly at this point, as the thinness of the application and the volatility of the product will mean that it will vaporize off at room temperature over a few minutes at the same time becoming hard."

"So how long do I have?" asked Sheeba.

"Ninety seconds at the most," said Shad. "I've timed it. And this is where you'll take a large chunk of that time."

He had turned the syringe upside down again so that the flat metal piece was now on the bottom and he lined it up with the lipped piece on the table. Slowly, very slowly he lowered it onto the lipped piece.

"You don't want to drop it onto this bed piece," said Shad. "You want to lower it slowly until it feels like it has found its place. Then you give it a very slight push to seat it securely before releasing the extractor from the back of it."

They all watched Shad perform the very steps he was speaking. When he had removed the extractor tool from the back of the metal plate, he put it down. Then he slid the mated metal piece towards him and onto his palm from off the table. He held it in his fingers and looked at it carefully. Then he showed it around to everyone with the back of the flat metal piece facing them.

"If there is any leakage of Anigloo around the edge and up the lip it's no good and we're done. That's why less is more when it comes to the Anigloo. You can see there is no Anigloo along the sides here," said Shad, as he showed them the mated metal pieces.

"How do you judge how much Anigloo to use?" asked Sheeba.

"Again, that takes finesse. Obviously, at the Animae factory this is all automated, so we're really working at the margins here."

"So you don't actually know that it'll work?" asked Rak.

Shad looked at him and grinned.

"I know it will work. We just have to be careful. Not to be overly dramatic but we've got one chance with this. However, I know we can do it. I think it sounds more scary than it is. Just take your time. Use less Anigloo than you think and it'll work. Want to give it a try?" Shad asked Sheeba.

Sheeba nodded. Shad handed her the extractor tool. Then he took out a couple of metal pieces from the bag, one flat piece and one lipped piece. He put the flat piece onto the lipped piece and it seated itself. He also took out a tube of fake Anigloo.

"Remember," he said. "Do as I say and not as I did. You want to open up your tube of Anigloo first."

Sheeba nodded. Shad put the flat piece onto the lipped piece and it slipped right onto it slowly until almost becoming one.

"OK," said Shad. "I think you're ready. Remember ninety seconds. Go."

Shad picked up his P-Mac which he used to time her. Sheeba lasered off the top of the Anigloo tube. She picked up the extractor tool and started to slowly lift off the flat metal piece. Seconds turned into what seemed like minutes before the flat piece came off quite suddenly after not seemingly moving for a long time.

Sheeba held the metal piece on top of the extractor tool after having transferred the tool to her left hand. Ny and Rak crowded around her, willing her on in thought. Ny snuck a look at Shad's P-Mac. Only thirty seconds had elapsed. It felt longer.

Sheeba picked up the small vial of fake Anigloo with her right hand which appeared to be her dominant hand from what Ny could tell. Slowly, with the patience of her craft, she started to bleed a thin trail of the glue around the outer edge of the metal piece as she slowly made her way into the center.

When she was finished she put down the tube and transferred the extractor back to her right hand. Then she turned it upside down and hovered it over the lipped piece on the table. Ny looked at the time. Sixty-seven seconds had elapsed.

Over the next several seconds, Sheeba slowly lowered the flat piece onto the bottom lipped piece. Her hand was as steady as a robot's. Once seated, she gave it the slightest push to ensure a good seal and then released the extractor from the back of the flat piece. She looked up at Shad with a furrowed brow.

"Eighty-three seconds," he said. "I'd like to try and get that below eighty seconds if only to give us a little more breathing room. Great job on your first attempt. I knew we had the right person to do this."

Sheeba smiled.

"Let's do a real test run," she said.

"I was just about to suggest the same," said Shad.

Rubber, Meet Road

❝ The gimbal sling is not quite ready," said Shad, "so this run is going to be the most challenging. If you can do it on this run, you'll have no problem tomorrow when we're all set up. But first, let's slide this metal board into the back and stick a few of the lipped pieces onto it."

Rak helped Shad slide a dull, gray metal rectangle into the back of the van. It was around forty-five kilograms and it slid smoothly over the top of the bed. Next, Shad got into the back and glued three of the lipped pieces about a hand's width apart onto the metal board.

"That should do it," he said, grabbing the bag of fake Anigloo and the bag of metal squares.

"One more just in case," said Sheeba.

Shad looked at her and grinned.

"As you wish," he said, and he glued a fourth lipped piece to the metal rectangle acting as the flat metal's bed.

Sheeba grabbed the extractor tool and they all climbed into Mr. T. There were four captains' chairs. Two facing the windshield and two facing the rear of the van. Clarity climbed into the driver's seat and Rak took the passenger seat. Shad took the captain's chair just behind his wife and Sheeba took the captain's chair just behind her husband. That left only a small bench along the passenger side for Ny to sit on. Clarity started up the engine. The van came to life and started to idle, vibrating ever so slightly.

"I didn't realize the van would vibrate so much," said Sheeba.

Shad nodded.

"You'll get used to it," he said. "Oh, you've also got the wrong tool. One minute."

Shad took the extractor from Sheeba and jumped out of the side of the van. He wasn't gone long. He returned with something that looked like an extractor tool but it had many more attachments. There was another tool that came along with it too. Shad handed them both to Sheeba.

"That one is just a gimbal-stabilized extractor tool. The other one is a gimbal-stabilized Anigloo tube holder. With these, the vibrations shouldn't worry you too much, if at all." He reached over and patted her knee. "You'll do fine. I have all the confidence in the world."

Ny believed him. He seemed confident and that gave them all confidence. Clarity started to drive towards the end of the hangar. There appeared to be another room there. Something that looked and reminded Ny of a garage for parking cars from a hundred and fifty years ago.

"This is very exciting," said Ny. "I've never been in a combustion engine vehicle before."

"Who else hasn't?" asked Shad.

"Not me," said Rak.

"Me neither," said Sheeba.

"And as a special treat," said Clarity, "to make it all the more fun, we'll play some A-Team shows as we drive around. There's a screen at the back for all of you in the back and there's this little one up front for Rak." Clarity tapped at the touchscreen panel between her and Rak in the front console.

A thin screen rolled down from the back of the van's roof and stopped halfway down the rear van doors. Shortly afterwards the opening monologue of that very old TV show started up.

"In 1972, a crack commando unit was sent to prison by a military court for a crime they didn't commit. These men promptly escaped from a maximum security stockade to the Los Angeles underground. Today, still wanted by the government they survive as soldiers of fortune. If you have a problem, if no one else can help, and if you can find them... maybe you can hire The A-Team."

The door to the room at the end of the hangar slid open and Clarity drove the van inside. The door slid closed behind them.

"OK, you probably all want to put on your air scrubbers. This van was hand built, so even though it has a main air scrubber to clean the air from the outside, it's not as tightly sealed as pods so let's just err on the side of caution."

They all put their air scrubbers on. Clarity checked from the rearview mirror. Then she tapped the screen on the P-Mac which was attached to the top of her dashboard. The outside door started to slide open. Outside the lights from the van showed you just how appalling the environment was. The light was yellowed by the soup that made up air. Ny shook his head subconsciously. This was why he was freeing El. Because she was humanity's last hope. If they succeeded, and if she decided to help them.

Ny turned around and started to watch the first A-Team show. He wasn't that familiar with the storyline other than he'd seen bits and pieces of a few of the series here and there. He knew the main characters by name and the over-arching theme which was told to you in the opening monologue. Still, it was better than watching the particulates suspended in the unbreathable air outside like tiny demons of doom.

Clarity turned left and headed back the way they had come. The going was bumpy on the dirt road before they made it onto the paved road.

"Don't be alarmed if you think someone's following us," said Clarity, "that's just our personal pod. Shad has it follow me whenever I take Mr. T out for a ride. He's worried that Mr. T will break down and leave me stranded. I guess you don't trust my mechanic skills, darling."

Ny saw her wink in the rearview mirror at Shad.

"Not true," he said. "I have every confidence, I just don't have all the confidence in the environment and the road conditions."

"The environment won't worry us, I've added an engine air scrubber. The engine is probably breathing cleaner air than we are," she said.

"Still, the last thing I want is you stranded on the road and waiting for help."

Time Master

They drove on for a while, giving Sheeba a feel for the vibration and swaying of the van they were in.

"This is about as steady as it'll get," said Clarity. "I'll try and keep the speed between seventy-five and eighty kilometers per hour."

"I didn't realize there was a speed limit on the roads," said Ny.

"There isn't. Well, there isn't for self-driving pods. But if you're driving a combustion engine vehicle or CEV, you have to pass a driving test. And part of that is that you need to know the speed limits. Maximum eighty on these highways and thirty-five within any populated areas," said Clarity.

"Wouldn't it be better to do this driving around the city then?" asked Sheeba.

"I don't think so," said Shad. "Firstly, you've got a lot more stopping and starting, and even with the most delicate drivers you'll find it more jerky. There's also a lot more twists and turns. Secondly, you're just that much closer to the jackboots which is an additional risk."

"But aren't we heading back towards the city?" asked Sheeba.

"The general direction, yes, but I imagine that Clarity will head south in a while before we get close to the city and do a big loop in this general area," said Shad.

"Exactly what I'll be doing," said Clarity.

Ny watched her drive. It was like something he'd only seen in the movies before. She had both hands on the steering wheel. If the steering wheel was an old-fashioned clock face, then her left hand was holding it where the number nine would be and her right hand where the three would be. Her right leg was pushing down on a pedal on the floor in front of her seat. Ny knew that to be the accelerator pedal. It made the vehicle go faster. To the left of that was another pedal that was to slow down the vehicle. Ny believed it was called the brake pedal. Clarity's eyes faced forward and watched the road ahead of her through the large windshield.

Ny could also see the speedometer on the dash in front of her steering wheel. It was analogue which by itself intrigued Ny. The needle that pointed to the speed like an hour hand pointed on a clock, was slightly right of what would have been the number twelve on the clock. The needle was pointing just to the left of a large white numbered fifty. Underneath that in smaller blue lettering you could see the number eighty.

"Why does the speedometer have two sets of numbers?" asked Ny.

Clarity looked up at him through the rearview mirror and smiled.

"The large white numbers are miles per hour. It was an archaic method of measuring speed that used to be used in these parts when it was still called the United States of America," she said.

Ny nodded. He'd heard of miles per hour from his movies and from history textbooks. Not that he'd paid much attention. It was like learning about the early telephone and rotary dialing. So old and archaic that it seemed irrelevant to him. And it was.

"I know, it's a little bizarre looking at it. I'm surprised they got as much done using imperial measurements as compared to metric. Metric's much better. In fact, the mile was originally from Rome where they called it 'mille passus' which literally means 'thousand paces'. That's how it was measured back then. By the time the twentieth century rolled around it had been standardized to the kilometer. And you can imagine why. A thousand paces measured by two different legs are different distances. More than that, it's probably really hard for the same pair of legs to measure the same distance when walking a thousand paces twice. Now the kilometer is a much better system. Built off of the meter which, as you know, is the distance that light travels in a specific fraction of one second."

Ny nodded. He was having the time of his life. Not so much with the history of distance measurement, but rather with the whole event. He was with his best friend. He was driving around in a pretty good-looking van and he was about to change humanity's destiny one way or another. If SAM ended up destroying humanity, well, Ny wouldn't be remembered at all. If SAM ended up helping humanity find its way again, there'd be songs sung about him. Or at the very least he'd have a statue. None of that was important. But it was exciting. He'd never felt so alive in his life.

"Why are you wearing leather gloves?" he asked her.

Clarity took her right hand off the steering wheel and looked at her gloved hand as she pivoted her hand back and forth. The gloves had little straps around the wrist that seemed to clasp at a stud-like button. There were also tiny holes all over the glove that looked put there on purpose, with slightly larger holes over the knuckles. The gloves were black.

"Well, they're not leather as you could probably guess. But these are driving gloves. They help keep the steering wheel in pristine condition but they're also very comfortable, and more than that, they offer greater grip and control of the steering wheel."

Ny nodded.

"OK," said Shad. "If we're all done with questions about driving and the van, maybe we can get to the task at hand."

He was grinning. Ny nodded.

"Why don't you give it a try, whenever you're ready?" said Shad, turning his head to his left and looking at Sheeba.

Sheeba got up and put her hand flat on the roof to stabilize herself as she stepped towards Ny and the middle of the van in front of the metal bed with the four lipped pieces.

"It'd be easier without the air scrubber," she said.

"I know, but just try and see beyond it. Tomorrow, you'll have a harness attached to the roof to keep you from stumbling. For now, Ny, would you mind holding her waist so that she doesn't fall down?" said Shad.

Ny put his hands up on each side of her waist. He couldn't keep her from falling if they lurched violently, but it was something to give her confidence in the vibrating and slightly swaying van.

"Let me know when you're ready," said Shad, "so I can time you."

Sheeba nodded. She took four flat metal pieces out of the bag and put them onto the lipped pieces where they seated themselves. Next, she took out a fake vial of Anigloo and lasered off the top of it. She took the extractor and placed the rubber end on the back of the first metal piece. She looked over at Shad and nodded.

"Go," he said.

Ny gripped her around the waist. Clarity kept the van as steady as she could. The one thing about the roads around here, was that being so close to Boise and VM's head office, the roads were in great shape. No potholes that she could see. The self-driving pods were constantly moving over the roads and sending data about the state of the roads to the Bureau of Movement who were pretty good at sending out road repairing machines to keep on top of it.

Ny couldn't see anything on account that Sheeba was blocking his view. He could watch the back of her arms and her elbows as she moved her hands ever so slightly.

"Twenty-seven seconds," said Shad. "Great time so far."

Ny saw Sheeba's elbows move. He couldn't tell that she had unseated the flat piece and was now holding it upside down on the extractor tool in her left hand. Sheeba picked up the fake vial of glue and started to bleed it along the outer rim, working towards the center.

The van swayed as it drove over a slight dip in the road. Sheeba paused before continuing on. A gust of wind buffeted the van which also caused her to sway. She had to take a step in order to prevent herself from stumbling. Ny held onto her for dear life. His arms were getting tired. Sheeba stepped back and steadied herself. She continued with the vial of fake Anigloo.

Ny looked at Shad. He was frowning at his P-Mac. Sheeba put the vial down and transferred the extractor to her dominant hand. She turned the extractor upside down so that the flat piece with the glue on it was now hovering above the lipped piece.

"Ninety seconds" said Shad. "I'm afraid you've run out of time."

Sheeba looked at him.

"Jupiter, Juno and Mars," she cursed. "Let me just seat this anyway and see if it would have even been a viable fit."

Sheeba took another several seconds to seat the flat piece onto the lipped piece. When she was done she looked up at Shad.

"Ninety-seven seconds," he said. "Take a break for a bit."

Sheeba turned around and put her hand on Ny's shoulder.

"Thanks for your support," she said. "It was really helpful."

"No problem, though my arms could use a break now too," he said, grinning.

Mother of Mars

Sheeba sat back down and Shad got up and knelt in front of the metal rectangular piece that had the lipped pieces on it. This large rectangular piece had been placed on top of what might have been a makeshift single bed opposite Ny. Shad took his P-Mac and scanned over the fitted metal piece that Sheeba had just recently glued. He stood back up and sat back down next to her. He looked at the P-Mac and then showed it to Sheeba.

"I'm afraid this one wouldn't have worked regardless," he said.

Sheeba nodded and twisted her mouth all into one corner of her face in disappointment.

"Mars dammit," she said. "I had a feeling it wasn't that good. Any suggestions?"

"Try and unseat the flat piece quicker," he said. "You're down to twenty-seven seconds so there's a lot of time to be taken on that portion of the task."

"I'm worried about taking it off too quickly. You said the real E3C is quite fragile," said Sheeba.

"It is, but I've determined that you have to really be putting a lot of pressure onto the back of it. If you can do it in ten to fifteen seconds you'll be fine. Try and aim for under twenty seconds this time."

Sheeba nodded.

"Let's wait until Clarity's turned the corner. How long, darling?" he asked her.

"It's just up ahead. Less than a kilometer."

"Can I have a look?" asked Ny, reaching out his hand toward Shad.

Shad leaned over and handed him the P-Mac. You could zoom in and see a close up image of the mated piece, but even without that, the schematics on the P-Mac identified the excess Anigloo leaking just off the rim of the lip by coloring it red. There wasn't a ton of excess Anigloo, but there were a few spots. Ny handed it back to Shad.

"Not a ton of red," said Ny.

Shad nodded.

"I know, a good job overall, especially for your first try in a moving van. Unfortunately, the tolerances are such that there cannot be any red if it's to work."

Ny and Sheeba nodded.

"Turn coming up," said Clarity.

The van slowed. Rak turned around and patted Sheeba on the shoulder.

"Good effort, sweetheart," he said. "You'll get this next time."

Clarity turned the van as slowly as she could. Ny barely swayed on the narrow bench he sat on that ran the length of the passenger side of the van from the back door to within about a meter of Sheeba's captain's chair. That wasn't to suggest that it was an extremely long bench. Less than two meters.

Ny swayed a little towards his left side, towards the back door, as Clarity pushed lightly on the accelerator to get back up to speed. Ny went back to watching the A-Team. The first episode of season one was about the A-Team trying to rescue a reporter who'd been kidnapped by Mexican outlaws. You'll have to watch it to see if they succeed.

"Up to speed," said Clarity.

Shad looked over to Sheeba.

"Whenever you're ready," he said.

Sheeba stood up and took a few steps over towards Ny. She turned and faced the large metal rectangle with the dummy E3Cs on it. Ny brought his hands back up towards her waist and tried to stabilize her as best as he could.

Sheeba took another vial of fake Anigloo out of the bag and lasered the top of it off. She grabbed her extractor tool and placed it just over the second small, flat metal piece. She looked over at Shad and nodded.

"Go," he said.

Ny let his head drop slightly so that he was looking at a spot between his feet and Sheeba's heels. Keeping his head held up while his arms were up and gripping the sides of Sheeba's waist was too much effort. He started counting off the seconds.

"Nineteen seconds," said Shad. "Great job".

Ny couldn't see it, but he imagined that Sheeba had detached the flat piece from the lipped piece. She held it upside down and transferred it to her left hand. She grabbed the fake Anigloo and took a breath to steady herself. She held it in. She started bleeding it around the edge, working towards the center now. The gimbaled Anigloo holder was helpful, it took away any slight shaking of her hand which couldn't be helped on account that she was in a van that was swaying slightly on the road and vibrating from the engine.

She transferred the metal piece back to her dominant hand and turned the extractor upside down again and hovered the piece over the lipped piece. She slowly started to let it down onto the lipped piece.

"Ninety seconds," said Shad. "Sorry."

"Mars dammit," said Sheeba. She finished what she was doing and went and sat back down. Shad got up and captured an image with his P-Mac as he did for the first one. He came back down and looked at it.

"Did it at least sit properly?" asked Sheeba.

Shad shook his head.

"I'm afraid not. Damn close though. Just one leaked bit of Anigloo."

Sheeba slapped her armrest with her right hand. Shad showed it to her, then he handed the P-Mac to Ny. It wasn't a bad job, just one small leaked bit of Anigloo highlighted red on the P-Mac's image towards one of the corners. Ny handed it back to Shad.

"You'll get it next time," said Ny.

Sheeba smiled at him.

"Let's take a longer rest," said Shad. "I think it'll be a few minutes before the next turn."

They sat in silence for a while, all thinking the same thing. What if Sheeba couldn't pull it off? Despite Ny's best wishes, he was the most worried. He didn't want to offer El up before he'd seen Sheeba nail at least one of these dummy E3C chips. And they only had two left.

"What happens if I can't do either of the next two?" Sheeba asked.

"Well," said Shad, "I really want to see you manage at least one. I think not only will it give all of us a great boost of confidence, but I'm not willing to take our one shot at creating SAM from Eve if you haven't managed to successfully seat one of these groups. And by these groups I don't mean from this group of four. If you can't do it with either of these next two, we'll head back and grab the rest of the pieces and line them up. We have dozens. Plus, we'll attach the harness for better stability."

"That might help," said Sheeba.

"It'll be a huge help," said Shad. "But I promise you. If you can nail either of these two without a harness, when you put the harness on, it's going to be like stealing candy from an Animae, if you'll forgive me for using that unkind expression."

Sheeba nodded, but Ny didn't see a lot of confidence in her face. They drove on in silence for a little while more. Ny watching the A-Team and grinning at the show.

"Turn coming up," said Clarity, and the van started to slow before taking another left turn. They continued to sit in silence, each one held captive by their own insecure thoughts about Sheeba's ability to pull this off.

"Up to speed," said Clarity. "You can do it, Sheebs, I know you can."

She grinned at Sheeba in the rearview mirror. Sheeba got up and patted Clarity's right shoulder.

"Thanks," she said.

She walked back to her usual spot between Ny and the large rectangle in front of her that held two more of her nemeses. Ny put his hands back up on each side of her waist. They were fatiguing more easily with each attempt. But he gripped her as firmly as he could. Sheeba shook her shoulders, took in and exhaled a large breath. She clapped her hands in front of her to give herself a boost of confidence.

"You can do it, sweetheart," said Rak, turning in the front passenger seat and craning his neck to see how she was doing.

"This is it," said Ny. "I can feel it in my bones."

"You've got this," said Shad.

"You go, superstar," said Clarity.

A small smile crept over Sheeba's face. She prepared the next vial of fake Anigloo and got herself setup.

"Maybe we can try it without any seconds counting," she said, looking over at Shad. He nodded.

"I'm ready," she said.

"Go," he said.

And Ny started counting up. He was at sixty-seven seconds when Clarity spoke.

"Shit," she said. "We've got company."

"Who is it?" asked Shad.

"The Mars damn jackboots," said Rak.

On the screen between Rak and Clarity flashed a notification that ordered them to pull over. A large flashing orange digital countdown was happening at the same time. It was at twenty-one seconds, twenty seconds and counting lower.

"I have to pull over," Clarity said.

"Give us as much time as you can," said Shad.

"That's only a few seconds."

Sheeba tried to ignore it but it had affected her confidence. She was hovering the metal piece over the lipped piece when the van started to slow and drift towards the right side of the road. The ticking of the signal light could be heard like the reminder of a clock.

"Time's up," said Shad.

"Mother of Mars," cursed Sheeba, as she seated the flat piece on the lipped piece and pulled away the extractor.

"Ninety-four seconds," said Shad. "Not bad."

"Second place is the first loser," said Sheeba, as she sat down heavily in her chair.

The countdown timer on the dash hit ten and the dash turned a pulsing red. The van would be disabled if the countdown hit zero. The jackboots had a variety of ways to do it. Thankfully, by the time the van stopped there was still seven seconds on the clock.

Don't miss out!

Visit the website below and you can sign up to receive emails whenever Jason Blacker publishes a new book. There's no charge and no obligation.

https://books2read.com/r/B-A-RBB-JTLBB

BOOKS 2 READ

Connecting independent readers to independent writers.

Also by Jason Blacker

A Lady Marmalade Mystery
Beggar's Pardon
Sins of the Father
Gandhi's Sorrow
Phantoms of the Pharaoh
The Baron at Bishops Avenue
The Priest at Puddle's End
Lady Marmalade Cozy Murder Mysteries: Box Set (Books 1 - 3)
Four Red Diamonds (A Lady Marmalade Mystery 4 Pack)
Heartless
Loose Lips
Misery's Company
Poisoned Heart

An Anthony Carrick Mystery
Fourth Wall
Fifth Estate
Sixth Sense
Seventh Son
Brotherly Love
Anthony Carrick Hardboiled Murder Mysteries: Box Set (Books 1 - 3)
First Feature
Money Ain't Nothing
All In

Four Ways to Midnight
Second Fiddle
Third Base
Washed Up

Carbon Heart Silicon Soul
Jupiter: Book 1
Juno: Book 2

Head Case Trilogy
Head Rush

TaXI Adventure
Ta.X.I. to Angola

Standalone
Can You Please Be Quiet
Dust on His Soul
Flowers For The Journey
Forever Famine
Livid Blue
My Son And I
Ruffled Feathers
Running Red River
When There Was One
Red Reign
The Enigma Evolution
Small Boy

Lady Marmalade Cozy Murder Mysteries: Box Set (Books 4 - 6)

Watch for more at JasonBlacker.com.

About the Author

Jason Blacker was born in Cape Town but spent most of his first 18 years in Johannesburg. When not grinding his fingers down to stubs at the keyboard he enjoys drinking tea, calisthenics and running. Currently he lives in Canada. Under his own name he writes hard boiled as well as cozy mysteries, action adventure, thrillers, literary fiction and anything else that tickles his muse. Jason Blacker also writes poetry and daily haikus at his haiku blog. You can find his haikus and other poetry at his website **www.haiqueue.com**. For FREE books and to stay up to date and learn about new releases be sure to visit **www.jasonblacker.com** where you can find more information about his writing and upcoming projects. If you enjoy space opera in the tradition of Star Trek then take a look at Jason Blacker's pen name "Sylynt Storme". It is under the name Sylynt Storme where you can find both sci-fi and vampire fiction written by Jason Blacker. "Star Sails" is the space opera series and "The Misgivings of the Vampire Lucius Lafayette" is his vampire series.

Read more at JasonBlacker.com.